EAST RENFREWSHIRE

D1580969

Maxwell's

Mega

Mission

For Rosie and Ty,
Ruaridh, Connel and Floraidh – JB

To Ruby and Liv – SG

Maxwell's
Mega
Mission

written by
Jayne Baldwin

illustrated by
Shalla Gray

Curlytale
Books

Contents

Chapter 1   In which Maxwell makes a discovery, and
moans about his Dad   6

Chapter 2   In which Dad mixes up Mitchell and and
Mackenzie again, and there's a surprise
for Maxwell.   11

Chapter 3   In which Maxwell and Dad go on a
mission for Mum.   17

Chapter 4   In which Maxwell learns an amazing
mouse trick.   25

Chapter 5   In which Maxwell discovers the source
of the terrible smell.   31

Chapter 6   In which Maxwell and Dad face death
by deadly claws.   35

Chapter 7   In which Maxwell teaches Morag the
amazing mouse trick.   41

Chapter 8   In which the centipede game is explained,
and Maxwell makes a confession.   48

Chapter 9   In which we find out why Morag hates
creepy crawlies, and Maxwell mentions
his mission.   59

Chapter 10   In which Maxwell makes a move.   67

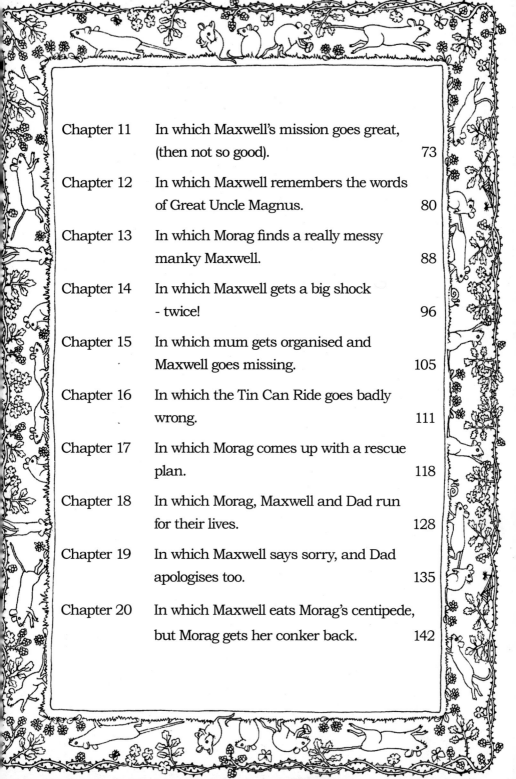

Chapter 11	In which Maxwell's mission goes great, (then not so good).	73
Chapter 12	In which Maxwell remembers the words of Great Uncle Magnus.	80
Chapter 13	In which Morag finds a really messy manky Maxwell.	88
Chapter 14	In which Maxwell gets a big shock - twice!	96
Chapter 15	In which mum gets organised and Maxwell goes missing.	105
Chapter 16	In which the Tin Can Ride goes badly wrong.	111
Chapter 17	In which Morag comes up with a rescue plan.	118
Chapter 18	In which Morag, Maxwell and Dad run for their lives.	128
Chapter 19	In which Maxwell says sorry, and Dad apologises too.	135
Chapter 20	In which Maxwell eats Morag's centipede, but Morag gets her conker back.	142

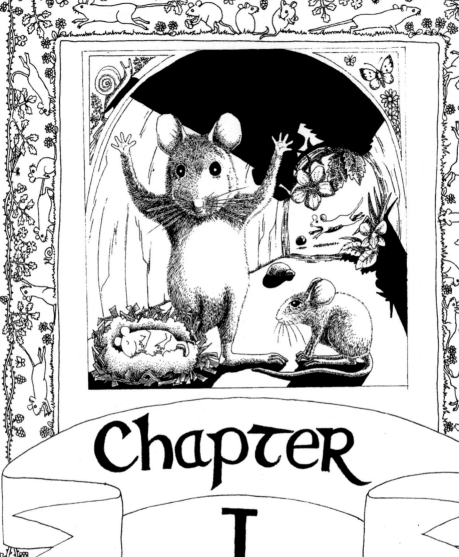

Chapter

I

In which Maxwell
makes a discovery,
and moans about his Dad.

"**Why** has the baby been called Mhairi?" Maxwell asked his mum.

"Because we like the name," she answered smiling down at the new addition to the family and giving her a little squeeze. Mhairi squeaked with happiness.

"I guessed that Mum," Maxwell added, in a voice that meant 'duh!', "I mean why have you called her something beginning with an M too."

Maxwell had only realised with the naming of his new sister that, in fact, they all had names beginning with M. He felt pretty stupid that it had taken him this long to realise, after all he was the eldest and had already seen the arrival of brothers called Mackenzie, Malcolm, Magnus, Mitchell and Murray and sisters Morag, Martha, Maisie and now Mhairi.

His Mum laughed, finally putting the now sleeping baby into the cosy nest that had been made to keep her safe and warm. "Your Dad and I like names beginning with an M. M stands for magnificent, marvellous, magic, munificent, magnanimous!" she said spreading out her arms dramatically with each word. Maxwell was glad she'd put the baby down. He was also sure she was making some of those words up; munificent, magnanimous, what on earth was she going on about.

"Well that's ok for you Mum but Dad begins with a D", Maxwell said. His Mum laughed again, "Yes but Dad and I have names too you know, I know we're Mum and Dad to you but our names are Murdo and Maggie Mouse. Anway, D stands for delightful, daring, dangerous..."

"Dull", chipped in Maxwell, who didn't think his Dad was daring at all.

"Now then, don't be cheeky and don't start going on about things being boring again." his Mum chided.

Maxwell mooched off to the part of the mouse house that he shared with his brothers, muttering as he went. "M doesn't stand for magic and munificent, whatever that is, it stands for mundane and, and, and...monotone," words he wasn't sure about but knew basically meant boring. To Maxwell just about everything was boring. His sisters had been excited by the arrival of baby Mhairi, even though she was pink and disgustingly bald, and even his younger brothers had become far too squeaky than he thought boys should be about babies. But for Maxwell it was just another dull thing about his dull, boring family.

Back in his room he found his brothers playing

marbles. "Honestly, even the games we seem to play begin with an M. Why can't we do something great, exciting, fantastic, brilliant, thrilling...MEGA," he said to himself as he sat grumpily in a corner refusing to take part in the game. That's what he wanted life to be — MEGA.

His Dad, home from fetching food, popped his head into the room. He smiled and asked the boys if he could join in. Maxwell watched as his Dad soon became excited as his marble pushed one of Mitchell's away from the big bull ball in the middle.

"Yes," said Dad, punching the air. As Maxwell groaned, "Oh for goodness sake," Dad caught sight of his eldest son sitting morosely in the corner.

"Come and join in Maxwell, this is great fun," he called, not noticing that as his back was turned Mitchell was attempting to put his marble back in place near the target. His brothers had seen this sly move though and Dad turned back as Mackenzie shouted, "cheater, cheater, cheater." Dad just laughed and tickled Mackenzie, then Mitchell, although it might have been Mitchell then Mackenzie, he still struggled to tell the twins apart. All the boys dived on Dad and made a heap of wriggling, tickling, laughing mice — but not Maxwell. He got up and stomped out of the room.

At the front hole of the mouse house he kicked Morag's favourite conker that she'd been told to leave outside. (She'd almost knocked her sister Maisie out the day before as she'd been throwing it around inside. It had ricocheted off the wall and cracked Maisie on the side of the head. She still had a lump and had cried for an hour. Mum had not been pleased.)

Maxwell went to sit on his favourite tree root and looked out across the long garden towards the small cottage in the distance. He could see the outline of the roof as the stars went out and the night sky began to lighten ready for the sun to rise. He jumped when he heard a voice say: "There you are, I wondered where you'd gone. Time for bed now son." Dad waited as Maxwell reluctantly climbed down. "Show an example to your brothers now won't you, and settle down quickly. Mum's cross with me for getting them all in a giddy pickle so close to bed time."

Chapter

2

In which Dad mixes up Mitchell
and Mackenzie (again), and
there's a surprise for Maxwell.

At breakfast next evening Maxwell got the distinct impression his Mum and Dad had been talking about him after he'd gone to sleep. There was something a bit odd about their conversation.

"While I'm feeding Maisie I do get extra hungry you know," Mum said to Dad.

"Of course you do, is there anything special you'd like me to get?" he replied.

Maxwell wondered what they were going on about. He didn't usually pay much attention to their conversations, they were very dull like everything else. Who Dad had seen while he was out, what the weather was like outside, was it a good year for fruit, had the old lady in the cottage sown any sunflowers. They just droned on and on and it was even worse if their friends came round. But this evening they seemed to be talking in a loud awkward way that had attracted his attention even over the top of the even more ridiculous arguing of his little brothers and sisters. "I sit there, I always sit there, no you don't, yes I do, you're sitting on my tail, no I'm not, yes you are," that sort of thing.

"Well," he heard Mum say, "I would quite like my favourite treat, if that would be possible sweetheart."

Mitchell made a noise as if he was being sick at the sound of this affectionate word.

"That's enough Mackenzie," Dad said. The kids all giggled. Dad still had trouble telling the twins apart.

"Yeh...that's enough Mackenzie," laughed Mitchell punching his brother. Seconds later the boys were made to put down their seeds and leave the room hungry.

Dad settled down again to finish his breakfast. "So what would that be my..." he was going to say another term of endearment like darling, or sweet cheeks but thought it best not to risk saying anything too slushy that might encourage an outburst from the remaining children.

"Cheese." Mum announced in reply.

There was a gasp from all the mouselets, including Mitchell and Mackenzie who were obviously only just outside the door waiting for a chance to sneak back in to finish their seeds. Their tummies were rumbling and all this talk of cheese was making it worse. None of the young mice knew where Dad got the cheese from and it was a rare treat. It was only in the really cold weather when the seed stores were getting low that Dad would come back with cheese or really tasty crumbs. They all knew that the store room was full to bursting now with seeds, nuts and fruit; so why was Mum asking for cheese?

During the evening the mouselets were allowed to play within a small area of the mouse hole; no further than they could run fast on one big breath was the rule. They weren't sure why, but Dad had told them they must always be able to dart back quickly down the mouse house's main hole. They had explored as far as they could, the older ones could range further than the younger ones, but no one had ever found any cheese growing.

Maxwell and his sister Morag, who was only just a bit younger than him, had always wondered if Dad bartered for it with others like Seamus Shrew, perhaps he grew cheese, or even old Hamish Hare. Maxwell had once seen him leaping about in the long grass; he looked like he knew how to grow all sorts of stuff.

"Anything for you my darling," Dad said immediately regretting the affectionate word he'd used as the retching noises were repeated by Mitchell and Mackenzie from the doorway.

"And do you think Maxwell is old enough to help

you now?" Mum added. Maxwell almost choked on his sunflower seed and Morag slapped him on the back just in case it had gone down the wrong way. So this was what the weird conversation was leading to he thought. He waited for Dad's reply but knew this had obviously been worked out earlier between them. Here it came.

"I think he just might be Mum. What do you think Maxwell?"

Maxwell was still struggling to swallow his mouthful whilst trying to stop Morag hitting him on the back but he began to nod frantically. Maybe, finally, life would become exciting, well at least for a little while.

"What about me, what about me, I'm only just a tiny bit younger?" Morag said stopping her thumping of Maxwell's back and tugging on her Dad's fur instead.

"No I'm sorry Morag, Dad can only cope with one of you at a time," Mum said adding, "You can help me with Mhairi today though." Morag did not look happy with that suggestion.

"Huh, I'd rather go watch the oak leaves dry," she grumped.

Maxwell jumped up when he finally forced down his mouthful. He was keen to go and he wanted to move away from Morag who looked like she was going to punch him again, but not on the back this time.

"When are we going Dad? Can we go now? Are we going like...like...now?" Maxwell was bouncing.

"Well I suppose so, no time like the present," Dad said. He was always coming out with these odd phrases. The mouselets looked at each other confused. Maxwell assumed that he meant yes.

"Come on then, come on Dad. Let's go then."

Maxwell saw Mum and Dad smile at each other. There had definitely been a plan he thought and although he wasn't sure why, he didn't really mind what they were up to as long as it meant something new and exciting for him. He was going with Dad to fetch cheese, from wherever cheese was fetched from and today was going to be new, today was going to be different. And it was just him, he didn't have to look after any of his brothers or his sisters. It was going to be just him and Dad. It had to be good.

Chapter

3

In which Maxwell and Dad
go on a mission for mum.

Maxwell scampered ahead of Dad out of the mouse house and darted across the litter of leaves that had fallen from the tree and now lay around the main entrance. They were dry and crispy now and they crunched noisily as he ran across them.

"Maxwell," his Dad hissed. Maxwell ran on too excited to stop, his Dad could catch him up he thought if he could run fast enough. He was over the leaves now and heading out towards the grass that ran down the middle of the garden. Suddenly he was grabbed by the scruff of his neck and dragged roughly to the edge of the grass.

"What's going on, gerroff, gerroff me," Maxwell squeaked. He was under the hedge at the side of the garden by the time he realised that it was Dad who had hauled him over. He was amazed his Dad had caught him so quickly, he didn't think he could move that fast.

"Maxwell!" his Dad was cross, he could tell. He wasn't shouting but his voice had an edge to it, very calm and serious. Maxwell waited quietly even though he was itching to get on with their mission.

"Maxwell," his Dad repeated, "Before we go any further we need to set some rules. I know you're excited son, and I don't blame you. I remember the first time your great uncle Magnus took me out. But there are dangers out here and I want you to learn about them from me, not the hard way."

Maxwell wasn't sure what his Dad meant by the phrase 'the hard way' but he thought maybe he should listen. He was sure his Dad was overreacting because his life was so dull. Was he worried Maxwell would be alarmed at running into a hedgehog, maybe he didn't know he'd already met one and all sorts of creatures they shared the wood with at the top of the garden?

"Are you listening to me son," Dad was saying when Maxwell realised he'd drifted off thinking about the robin he'd met recently when he'd managed to stay up far too late and it had been almost light outside.

"Yes Dad," he quickly answered.

"I need you to stay close to me. You have no idea where we're going so I don't know what you were thinking running ahead like that. You could have been going in the completely wrong direction."

Maxwell accepted this was true. He had no idea where the cheese could be growing or what it would look like; it could grow like a strawberry on the ground, or like an apple up a tree, or like a mushroom in the dark or a carrot in the earth. His Dad did have a point, he reluctantly accepted.

"We're going to the cottage," his Dad said. Maxwell was stunned. So stunned he even gasped. Wow, this really was going to be a mission for Mum, he thought, all the way to the bottom of the garden to the cottage. Maybe the Old Lady grew cheese inside somewhere instead of in her vegetable plot.

"Yes, the cottage," his Dad seemed to be pleased that Maxwell was impressed by the news, "and there are many dangers there and one in particular." He paused for dramatic effect. "A cat."

"O...K..." Maxwell said slowly not really sure what this was.

"Oh Maxwell," his Dad said in an exasperated tone, "a cat."

Still nothing from his son's blank face. "I blame myself," he said," we should have talked to you before now. I think we need to sit down when we get back and have a mouse to mouse chat about all the dangers we face. You're maybe old enough now to know why I was brought up by my Uncle Magnus and not my Mum and

Dad but now isn't the time. You must understand this though, the cat is deadly."

A look of fear fleetingly passed over Maxwell's face but then he wondered if his Dad was, as usual, exaggerating and a cat was actually no more deadly than the annoying spikes in a blackthorn bush.

"Maxwell this is serious." His Dad tried to weigh up what to say and realised he should have rehearsed this. He didn't want to frighten the living daylights out of his son but he did need him to understand.

"The Old Lady has a cat. At this time of the evening she should be asleep by the fire or on the Old Lady's lap, so we should be fine. But she can really hurt you." Maxwell noticed a catch in his Dad's voice and he stopped speaking for a moment. Then Dad said: "Cat's are evil, nasty creatures and they sneak up on you. You've heard Mum and I say 'as quiet as a cat'."

Maxwell couldn't recall that one. He switched off a lot when they were talking. The phrases most familiar to him were: 'you're as noisy as a nest of baby birds,' or 'you're as cheeky as a chaffinch.'

"Well, just do what I say, be very quiet and keep close to me," Dad said. "Now let's go, it's a dark night but it's

21

still best to keep under the hedge until we get down to the cottage."

Maxwell wasn't sure what difference the light meant only that they were all told to play close to the house when there was a full moon. He began to realise that there was a lot his Mum and Dad knew about things that they had never talked about in front of the mouselets. He followed as Dad set off again, scurrying over roots, under branches and around rocks and stones. There was a far off screech at one point and his Dad flattened suddenly to the ground so Maxwell did the same. It seemed like ages before his Dad moved on again.

"Owl," his Dad said mysteriously. "That's something else to tell you about when we get home."

They scurried down the length of the garden, keeping under the hedge where they could. Maxwell stayed close to his Dad, stopping when he stopped and watching as his Dad looked about, his ears swivelling back and forth and his whiskers twitching as he sniffed the night air. Two steps led down from the edge of the grass and on to an area of stone slabs, big flat ones, that lay between the grass and the wall of the cottage. While Dad was doing his sniffing and ear swivelling Maxwell looked at the cottage and he could see it had a large wooden door with what looked like a smaller door at the bottom of it.

"Is that a little door for us Dad?" Maxwell said, impressed that the Old Lady seemed to have thought of them. Dad's eyes widened like daisies opening in the sun and he looked at Maxwell as if he'd never seen him before. He slapped his forehead with his forepaw as he closed his eyes.

"Maxwell," he said very slowly and quietly, almost hissing, "that," he pointed at the flap, "that, is not for us you foolish little mouse. That is for Professor Whiskerton. THE CAT."

Maxwell gulped loudly, shocked at his mistake.

"What's a professor?" he asked finding his voice again.

"We don't have time for this son," said Dad, "but basically professor means she's very clever."

Maxwell was impressed but he thought he'd better check something: "And we don't want to meet this cat, right ?"

"We do NOT want to meet this cat or any cat." replied Dad shuddering at the thought. "Now listen, we have to

23

get across to the cottage, we're going to dash as fast as we can using the flower pots as cover. Follow me."

And with that Dad scooted across to the first plant pot he could see and then pressed himself back against the clay as he looked out to check the coast was clear. Maxwell dashed after him keeping as close to the pot as he could. The clay felt cold and damp against Maxwell's fur and he shivered, but Dad had sped on and Maxwell struggled to keep up as they darted and dashed from pot to pot. Dad scrambled across the final gap and reached the cottage wall. And disappeared.

Chapter

4

In which Maxwell learns
an amazing mouse trick.

Maxwell stared into the black night hoping that his Dad would reappear. All the noises of the night suddenly seemed really loud and he had no idea what most of them were. He didn't know whether to run across the last gap to see if he could find Dad or whether something had happened to him over at the cottage wall. Maybe the cat was lurking in the dark?

Maxwell could hear his own heart beating really loud, as if it was crashing off the walls of his rib cage. He was still frozen to the spot wondering what to do when he heard his name being hissed.

"Maxwell, are you coming or not?"

To Maxwell's astonishment it was Dad, now just at the spot where he'd last seen him next to the cottage wall. He scurried across the paving stone to where Dad was waiting. "But...but...but where did you go Dad? You just went, gone, disappeared."

"Into the cottage, I thought you were going to follow me but I waited at the other side of the wall and you didn't come. What were you doing?"

"What was I doing?" spluttered Maxwell, "I didn't know where you'd gone. I thought maybe that cat you'd mentioned had got you. What do you mean you waited on the other side of the wall?"

26

But instead of answering, his Dad once again disappeared. Maxwell just caught sight of the end of his long tail as it seemed to go into the wall itself. As Maxwell peered after him he saw the smallest gap in the stonework. He was still staring at it when his Dad reappeared, first the tip of his nose and whiskers and then he seemed to suddenly be there again.

"What are you doing son?" his Dad said now somewhat exasperated.

"Whoah Dad! How are you doing that?" Maxwell said a little too loudly, "That's just the teeniest gap, Dad, I don't know how you're making yourself so small. It's a bit gross. I can't get in there and I'm a lot smaller than you." Maxwell gazed at the tiny space between the stones in the cottage wall.

"Of course you can do it," his Dad whispered, "it's something we mice are really good at. It's a special talent we have, we can get through the smallest spaces, we can flatten ourselves and squeeze through tiny gaps. Just follow me."

Maxwell thought his Dad's only special talent was being able to bore you to sleep, but nevertheless he saw him, once again, disappear into the wall. Worried

27

his Dad would get really cross if he didn't try he went towards the space and began to work his way through. By pushing his nose into the gap he found to his amazement that his body changed and adapted to the space as it got smaller. It felt very weird and he was just wondering if he really wanted to carry on with it when he suddenly popped out of the other side. He was about to shout 'wow Dad I did it' when he felt his Dad's forepaw over his nose. He put one finger up to his own mouth to indicate that Maxwell should be quiet.

It was much warmer on this side of the wall and the smells in the air were completely different to anything he'd smelt before in the garden or the wood. It seemed darker too and it took a few moments before Maxwell's eyes got used to the change. There was a fabulous smell coming from somewhere close and his whiskers twitched wildly as he sniffed the air. He wanted to ask Dad if this was where the Old Lady grew the cheese because something really good was very close to them. Dad gestured that he should follow him and they set off keeping tight to the edge of the floor, the wall on one side. Maxwell was scampering along when he suddenly crashed into Dad, his long nose crumpling into Dad's bottom. Before he could say "yuck" his Dad turned, looking a little cross, but pointing at the crumbs Maxwell could now see just ahead.

Dad began to hurriedly pack as many crumbs he could comfortably manage into his cheek pouches and Maxwell copied him. Finally they picked up a lump of cheese each and began to retrace their steps. As Maxwell's eyes had become accustomed to the darkness he could see much better on the way back. And just near the place where they had first come in he could see where the wonderful smell was coming from. Near the small gap in the wall that had been their entrance and would now be their exit was what looked like an old tin can.

A shiny can with paper round it had landed once in the woods, not far from the mouse house and for a while Maxwell, Morag and the twins had played in it. It had been great fun, especially nibbling at the food that had been left in the bottom. But Dad had stopped them after Mitchell cut himself on a sharp bit. Maxwell wondered why there was a tin can lying there in the Old Lady's kitchen, maybe she'd dropped it and her eyesight wasn't very good, after all she'd left this cheese lying about. He remembered Great Uncle Magnus hadn't been able to see very well before he went away. If it happened to old mice, maybe it happened to old people too.

Maxwell thought there must be some food left in this tin can too because he could smell the best smell he had ever found wafting into his nose. He was transfixed, he just couldn't get enough of it. He wanted to stay there and concentrate on smelling it, it was that good and maybe he could find out what it was. But Dad was behind him and he pushed him forward. Maxwell was just trying to get a really big sniff of the great smell when suddenly something else appeared in his nose, another but very different even stronger smell. This smell didn't drift into his nose like the tangy aroma of cheese or softly like a freshly ripening strawberry, it arrived with a crash and a whoosh, like being hit on the nose by Morag's best conker, it made his eyes smart. And it didn't smell good at all. It was like the smell when Maisie had been sick or Magnus's poo had gone really runny after he'd eaten the rotten old bramble by mistake and he hadn't made it outside to the toilet nook in the tree. There had been a bad, stinky smell in the mouse house for days after that. This was a smell like that, a really strong stench, a really pooey pong. What could it be?

Chapter

5

In which Maxwell discovers the source
of the terrible smell.

Maxwell realised that he didn't really want to know where this new smell came from. There was something about it that made his hair stand on end and he wasn't sure why. And yet at the same time he found himself wanting to look round but Dad was pushing him forward. He'd dropped his cheese.

"CAT, CAT, CAT..." Dad shouted urging Maxwell to move. But Maxwell seemed to be fixed to the spot, stuck between the really great smell and the really bad smell. He slowly began to turn his head, wanting to see where the awful smell came from and yet not sure he really did. But before he could see anything he finally realised that Dad was prodding him hard and shouting that they were in danger.

"GO, GO, GO," he could hear. Finally making himself move he pushed his nose forward into the gap and squeezed through, feeling his body change again, then popping out of the other side. Dad was right behind him. Before Maxwell could drop his cheese to speak Dad was urgently urging him forward again.

"Move Maxwell move. Follow me fast now, now, NOW!"

Maxwell saw Dad run faster than he'd ever seen

anything move before, faster even than his brother Magnus when a big hairy spider had appeared behind him. Maxwell didn't like spiders either but at least he hadn't squealed and run away like a big pinkie baby. But he was running now, he thought he caught a whiff of that bad smell again somewhere near and he dashed after Dad who was darting between the flower pots ready to run under the hedge.

Dad didn't stop, and Maxwell didn't stop either. It wasn't easy running so fast with the cheese still between his teeth but after all this effort he wasn't going to drop it. His legs were getting tired and there seemed to be far more big sticks and stones in his path than there had been on the way down the garden. Maxwell could see that Dad kept glancing back to check he was still with him. He didn't know if the source of the terrible smell was following, but he certainly wasn't going to stop to look. The fact that they were in terrible danger had finally sunk in.

Maxwell had been focusing so hard on keeping up with Dad and following his every leap and swerve that he wasn't sure where they'd got to in the garden but he hoped they couldn't be far from home. But then that horrible stenchy stink came into his nose again and Dad suddenly disappeared into a small crack between two large rocks, part of the garden that seemed to be full of big stones. Maxwell followed him quickly into the darkness and immediately ran into Dad. There wasn't much room in this tiny little hole between the cold rocks. Dad dropped his cheese and Maxwell did the same, both of them were gasping for breath after running for so fast and for so long, their sides heaving. As their breathing began to calm down there seemed to be a little bit more space, but not much. Maxwell opened his mouth to ask why they'd run into this tiny hole when they must be so near home but Dad clamped his forepaw over his mouth again. A moment later Maxwell understood why. The very, very bad smell seemed to be seeping into the small space they were in, leaking in through the gap between the rocks. Something was outside, something horrible, something very scary, something very dangerous.

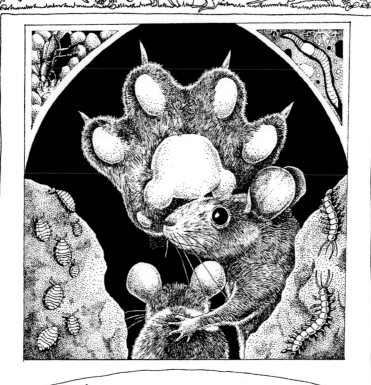

Chapter

6

In which Maxwell and Dad
face death by deadly claws.

Maxwell felt he could hardly breathe. Dad had made him wriggle backwards as far as he could go, which wasn't very far but it left a bit of a gap between them and the gap they'd sneaked in through. They could see the sliver of night, slightly lighter than the dark of the hole, but as they watched, it went black too and the terrible smell became so strong that Maxwell felt sick. They could hear the sound of something sniffing just outside. Maxwell was so scared he thought he would have been shaking like quakey grass if there had been enough room in this tiny space but he and Dad were wedged together between the rocks. They were not going anywhere.

Just when Maxwell thought that things couldn't get any worse, they did. A big hairy paw filled with sharp claws swept through the gap trying to catch anything within reach. Maxwell and Dad both instinctively drew their heads back. The claws missed them but only by a whisker and if the cat reached any further towards them there was nothing they could do, there was nowhere to go.

They listened. Maxwell didn't think he'd ever listened this hard before. In fact he was used to trying to turn his hearing off so he that didn't have to hear Mhairi's crying or the endless squeaking of Murray and Martha. "What's this Mum, what's that Dad, what're you doing Maxwell?" He wished he could hear them now, he wished he was at home, he thought he would never complain again about the silly chatter of his little brothers and sisters.

Now he was listening so hard he thought he could hear the scurrying of beetles and even the smooth sliding of a worm nearby. But most of all he could hear the quiet, soft, steady breathing of what he realised must be the cat. There was a slight hum to the breath, a soft rolling sound as she breathed in and breathed out. It made him feel whoozy, a bit sleepy, as if his head was filled with the tufty tops of cotton grass. He wanted to ask Dad what Professor Whiskerton was doing, he assumed it was the Professor, but he knew Dad would be really angry if he spoke. He was worried that if he could hear Professor Whiskerton breathing then perhaps she could hear them too?

Suddenly there was another swipe as the paw swept past their noses so close that Maxwell could feel the whoosh in the air. A claw caught the very tip of his nose and he wanted to cry out at the sharp pain but he knew he had to be very brave. He felt tears welling up in his eyes and his breath juddered as he tried to stop himself from crying. He tried to pull his nose back even further and they waited for the next strike, could she reach any further? If a scratch on the tip of his nose hurt this much, how much would it hurt if she managed to catch something else with her nasty sharp claws. They waited, and waited and the soft rolling sound of the cat seemed to fill their tiny hiding place, the humming noise reverberating off the rock walls. Maxwell felt as if a bumble bee had flown inside his ear and was now filling his head making it impossible for him to think straight but at the same time it was so soothing making him feel very, very tired.

It was only when Maxwell woke up that he realised that he'd been asleep. He couldn't believe he'd fallen asleep when he was so scared but he wondered if that humming sound the cat had made had caused his eyes to close. Maybe it was just that so much time had passed that he had simply nodded off in the darkness and stillness of the hole. He realised that the smell had gone now and he wondered why Dad hadn't woken him so they could set off home. The cat must have given up trying to catch them. So much time had passed that he could see that it was starting to get light outside. And then he realised he was alone, Dad wasn't there next to him.

Maxwell began to panic. Where was Dad? Had the Professor got him? How could he have slept through his Dad being snatched by the deadly claws? Maybe he'd fainted through shock. He could feel his heart beating so hard again he thought it might burst out of his chest when suddenly Dad rushed in through the gap.

"Dad, Dad," Maxwell cried, he'd never been happier to see anyone in his whole life.

"It's ok Maxwell," his Dad panted, "the cat's gone. I had to go and check but it's ok." He stopped again to catch his breath. "Sometimes you think a cat's gone but they're just waiting for you, quietly, so quietly, sitting there patiently waiting to pounce." Dad shivered and for a moment he had a sad, faraway look in his eyes as if he was remembering something.

"But's it's ok," he said bringing himself back from his thoughts, "the cat has definitely gone but we still need to be very, very careful and quick. It's getting light now and there are more dangers than cats and owls. Stay close son, you're doing really well. It's not far."

Maxwell picked up his cheese and slowly moved his legs. They were very stiff from being still in such a cramped space for so long. They felt funny too, all tingly. It took a moment before he could get himself moving again and then he had to run as Dad was scampering over the dew drenched grass, dashing towards the hedge and then up the garden towards home.

Maxwell managed to get his legs going but he struggled to keep up with Dad. He wished he could just grab Dad's long tail and be dragged along, but at the moment he thought he couldn't move any more, he saw the happy sight of home and Dad's tail disappearing inside the mouse house. With his last bit of energy Maxwell almost threw himself through the main hole and ran straight into Dad who had collapsed gasping just inside the entrance. Trying to catch his breath Dad managed to say quietly, "Well done son."

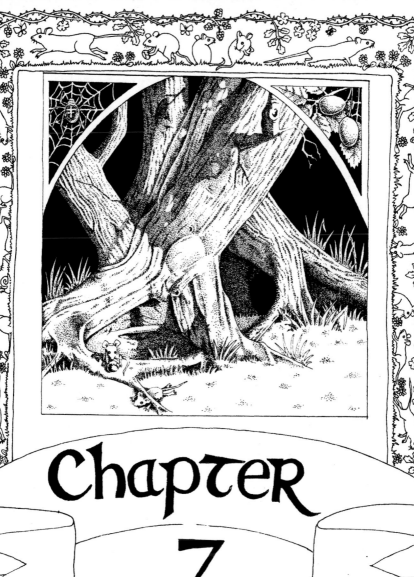

Chapter 7

In which Maxwell
teaches Morag the amazing
mouse trick.

The next evening Maxwell felt amazing even though he'd been so tired when he got home. His brothers had been bursting with questions when he got back and now over breakfast his sisters had a million more. Dad had told him not to say too much, there were things he felt the little ones shouldn't know about yet, like Professor Whiskerton. Maxwell had loads of questions to ask Dad too, like why did that cat smell so awful and what was the great smell and the tin can thing he'd seen? He also wanted to know how the cat had become a professor? He'd met Dr Dormouse when Mitchell had torn his ear on a bramble thorn but that was the cleverest creature he'd come across. But Dad had told him to try and get some sleep after he'd let him eat a tiny piece of the precious cheese they'd managed to bring back.

"Another time," was all he'd said in answer to some of the questions Maxwell had blurted out when he got his breath back from that final run. He'd seen Mum's face appear from the room she shared with Dad looking very worried so he'd gone to bed and despite the persistent pestering of his brothers they'd all soon been overcome by sleep.

"Settle down, settle down," Dad said now over the

squeaking of all the little voices as Maxwell's sisters bombarded him with questions. "Let Maxwell have his breakfast, and you all get on with yours."

Maxwell didn't feel very hungry, he was so excited about his mission with Dad that he had already begun to forget about how frightened he'd felt. He hoped he could get some answers from Dad too. What was the great smell? It had to be something to eat, it smelt so... well, tasty, even better than cheese Maxwell thought.

Mum had been late coming in for breakfast as baby Mhairi had been up most of the day, not letting Mum get much sleep. She looked tired, and although she smiled at Maxwell and thanked him for the cheese he felt there was something about her that was not quite right. Behind the smile he thought she looked...well, he wasn't too sure but definitely worried. He thought he saw Mum and Dad exchange glances.

He'd managed to escape all the questions after breakfast as Mum had said his brothers and sisters had to tidy up while she coped with the baby. He was sitting outside on his favourite root gazing at the little twinkling lights in the velvet black of the sky when his sister joined him. She'd come out to try and find the conker that Mum had banned her from taking into the hole when she spotted Maxwell.

"So," she said sitting down next to him, "how was it really? Don't give me that guff you were giving the others. Dad obviously told you not to say too much, I can tell Maxwell so don't try and deny it."

Maxwell didn't know what to do, Dad had told him not to say too much but this was Morag, she wasn't much younger than him and he knew she was really fed up that he'd been taken on the adventure and not her. Also, he was just bursting to tell someone how amazing it had been, how scary and exciting and how Dad had run much faster than he thought he could and how Dad knew loads of stuff about things he'd never talked about before.

"You mustn't let on to Dad that I've told you," Maxwell said putting on his very serious voice, "I mean it, swear on your conker." He confessed to Morag where he'd kicked it and when she brought it back she put her forepaw on the shiny chestnut and promised that she wouldn't tell. "Never, never, not ever," she added hoping this would persuade her brother to tell her everything.

And so Maxwell began to describe how Dad had said

there are loads of things that are dangerous that he hadn't told them about, like cats and owls and probably other stuff too. And how there was a special flap in the back door of the Old Lady's cottage that's just for her cat, a cat that's so clever it's called Professor Whiskerton, though he didn't know why.

"And the coolest thing," Maxwell said, "is how we mice can make ourselves really small or really flat to get though the tiniest spaces you've ever seen. It's amazingly weird, it feels strange, even your bones kind of move about like they're made of mushrooms or moss or something squidgy."

Morag looked at him as if he'd gone mad. "Yeah right," she said, "and worms can fly."

"No, really it's true," Maxwell said realising the only way to convince her was to do it. He looked about for a small space and found that next to the root they were sitting on was another that had lifted out of the earth a bit and left a small gap underneath. He jumped down and looked through to check it did open out again at the other side.

"Watch," he said. And with that he pushed his nose into the gap just as he'd done with Dad. It wasn't like

45

the stone of the cottage, he could feel the soft earth give way a little beneath him making the gap a bit bigger but it was still a squeeze. Once through, he popped his head over the root to see what Morag thought of that. She was stood with her mouth open, her nose twitching up and down as she looked at the gap and then up at Maxwell who was grinning from ear to ear.

Finally she said; "Wow!"

"Told you it was awesome, try it. It takes a bit of getting used to and it feels very strange and squishy but just point your nose in the hole and...well, push," Maxwell said.

Morag hesitated for a moment, what if it was only male mice that could do this, what if she tried and got stuck? Then she told herself that was silly, female mice could do anything male mice could do and more. And with that she approached the gap, which she was relieved was a little bigger now. In no time she was next to Maxwell on the other side of the root.

"That is just brilliant Maxwell!" she exclaimed.

They would have spent the whole night squeezing through small spaces but they had to stop when the younger ones came out to play. Maxwell thought Dad would be really cross with him if he told them about it before they were old enough to know. He also liked the fact that it was a something Dad had only shared with him, and now it was a secret between him and Morag.

They spent so long playing this new game that Maxwell forgot to tell Morag about the amazing smell and the old tin can that was lying on the kitchen floor. The smell had seemed to come from the can and he couldn't understand why Dad hadn't let him go and see if there were any scraps left inside it. There had to be, and they had to be really, really good if they tasted as good as they smelled.

Chapter

8

In which the Centipede
Game is explained, and
Maxwell makes a confession.

It was about a week later when the novelty of playing the squeezy game with Morag — only when the little ones weren't out — had worn off that Maxwell realised he was getting bored again. Bored, bored, bored.

He hadn't managed to get Dad on his own so he hadn't been able to ask all the questions that were still buzzing about in his head and keeping him awake at night, along with one or two nightmares about being chased by giant sharp claws. The scratch on his nose had healed up, even though he'd picked at the scab more than once. Dad had told him to say he'd run into a rose bush, and he'd kept his promise not to say what had really happened, not even to Morag or Mum.

Dad seemed to have been very busy since their adventure and he'd caught both Mum and Dad looking very worried. Maxwell knew Mum was tired, he'd heard Mhairi crying during the day when he'd been lying awake thinking about the cat and the smell and the can. When Dad did have time to play it was always with them all, playing hide and seek or marbles. Maxwell felt he was too old for these games now, Morag did too but she joined in to help with the youngest ones. The only time Maxwell had joined in was when Dad had surprised them all with a game of hunt the centipede, which was Maxwell's favourite.

Everyone had to start outside the house and Dad would release the centipede he'd captured in through the entrance hole. They all counted to ten and then scrambled after the creature. It sometimes took ages to find it and catch it. Centipedes move very fast, especially when they're running for their lives. Whoever found and caught the insect could eat it, but it was often a tie and several of the young mice would fight over the wriggling, squirming multi-legged mini monster, and sometimes it got away in the confusion.

The mouse house was very old, it had first belonged to Maxwell's great grandfather Malcolm, so there were lots of rooms and passageways, many that they didn't use anymore. It was very easy for a superfast centipede to escape down one of these dark old cobwebby holes so the mice had to run fast. Mum had once banned them all from playing for a while after Magnus and Maisie disappeared down one of the maze like routes in the oldest section and it had taken ages to find them. Magnus had been pretty shaken up, he swore he'd seen a spider so big he could see each of its eight eyes staring at him, but Maisie had stuffed herself silly with all sorts of bugs and creepy crawlies she'd found, to the point where she was horribly sick.

Maxwell had spent ages looking at what Maisie had thrown up as he was sure he could see all sorts of odd eyes, feelers and munched up shells in it. He also swore he'd seen some of the legs still twitching and claimed that was why Maisie had been sick — some were still alive in her tummy and had tickled her insides. Maxwell had reminded her of this for days afterwards as he loved the effect his teasing had on the little ones, they squealed and wriggled at the thought. But Mum had become very angry with him in the end as she said Magnus would never recover from his 'traumatic experience'. Maxwell wasn't sure what that was but Mum had told him to think about it one night instead of having supper. He'd sat in his room grumbling as his tummy rumbled.

In the end Dad had made a deal with Mum about the centipede hunt game, that the children could only chase the multi-legged bug within the area they lived in now. If it managed to escape beyond that then they just had to let it go.

Maxwell spent a lot of time sitting on his root gazing

back down the garden, out from the copse of trees where their home was, and down past the shrubs and grass, the vegetable plot and the rock garden to the cottage. He would watch as the Old Lady obviously went to bed and turned the lights out one by one. If only Dad would take him down to the cottage again, he wished. He thought that Dad would have at least taken him out foraging. Surely he was big enough now to help Dad find food, but the most he'd been asked to do was help move supplies from the entrance hole into the store rooms. If there was a lot of stuff, Dad asked Mitchell, Mackenzie and Morag to help too so it was nothing special really.

He was sitting on his root one night when Morag came and sat with him.

"Want to play squeezy for a while before the wee ones come out?" she asked but Maxwell wasn't interested any more. "Go on," she urged him but Maxwell couldn't be budged and it wasn't much fun by herself, though she did practice alone sometimes as she wanted to be the best at it.

"Come on Maxwell," she said, a bit fed up now with her moody brother, "what's the matter?"

Maxwell decided to tell Morag about the things he'd

left out or not got round to telling her on that first night they'd talked about his adventure.

"When I went out with Dad," he began. Morag pricked up her ears, she'd suspected there was more to their mission than Maxwell had let on.

"In the cottage there was an amazing smell... like whatever was making the smell was made of all your favourite things to eat rolled into one. Like sycamore seeds and acorns and mushrooms and centipedes all mashed together," Maxwell said with a kind of dreamy look on his face.

Morag thought this sounded horrible. She didn't particularly like centipede. She'd been the first to find the insect one night when Dad had brought one back to play the hunt the centipede game with and she'd hated the way it wriggled and tickled in her mouth as she tried to swallow it. Dad had told her to crunch it to make it stop struggling but she didn't like the way it was all soft and slimy inside and the legs still twitched. Yuck. It made her feel ill just thinking about it. Some of the others loved them, they said they tasted like a hazelnut on the outside and an over ripe strawberry on the inside. But it had reminded her of a seed she'd once tasted that had gone bad in the middle. The whole thing was horrible. After that she'd made sure that if she was the first one to find the centipede she let it go again, sometimes sneaking it back outside so it could go free and live another day. To get rid of the thought of centipede she turned her mind to what she thought tasted good.

"You mean like cheese and beechnuts and rosehips," Morag suggested thinking of how great it would be to have all those things mashed up together.

"Yeh, whatever," said Maxwell, thinking that sounded pretty yucky. "But even better somehow. And the smell seemed to come from a tin can, you remember that one we found? Dad told us it was a tin can and it had probably been in the Old Lady's rubbish, but it had fallen out somehow and ended up near us."

Morag remembered and nodded now at Maxwell, eager to hear the rest of the story. But as soon as he spoke again she wished she hadn't heard.

"I'm thinking of going back, on my own, to see what was in the can in the house, to find out what's making that great smell," Maxwell announced. Morag was stunned.

"What?" she spluttered. "You can't be serious. You've been with Dad once and you think you can go again on your own. You're crazy. I know there's something you're not telling me too Maxwell. I know that cat you told me about..."

"Professor Whiskerton."

"Yeah, Professor Whiskerton," she added. "I know she nearly caught you and Dad. I think she had something to do with that scratch on your nose. And I know something else."

It was Maxwell's turn to be stunned now and eager to hear what his sister had to say. How did she know about the close encounter with the cat? And what else did she know and how did she find it out, whatever it was?

"Well, what is it?" Maxwell finally said, exasperated after waiting for what seemed like ages for Morag who was looking a little smug. "What do you know, tell me, tell me, tell me?"

Morag took a deep breath wondering where to begin. "I overheard Mum and Dad talking the day after you got back. They thought we were all out playing but I'd popped back to get something from my room," Morag began, "it was my conker, you remember you told me where you'd hidden it and we used it to make the promise not to tell, well I'd been sneaking it inside after that in case you or Mitchell or Mackenzie were tempted to hide it again 'cos I know..."

"Morag!" Maxwell shouted, frustrated that she was giving him far too much information about stuff he didn't want to know about and nothing about what he did want to know about. "Please, just tell me the stuff about Mum and Dad."

"Oh, yes, ok," Morag said, a little put out that he wasn't that interested in how she'd managed to sneak the conker into the mouse house. "Well, I stopped to listen 'cos Dad was saying that you'd had to squeeze into his bolt hole..."

"Bolt hole?" Maxwell asked. "We did squeeze into a little gap in the rocky bit, but what's a bolt hole?"

"It's a place Dad knows he can can use to escape from the cat or any other danger if he has to, if he can't get home. He's got quite a few, all over the place," Morag explained.

"How do you know that?" asked Maxwell again, still amazed at how Morag knew all this stuff.

56

"Because I heard Mum asking which one you'd had to use and Dad had said 'not the one by the birch tree, or the old sparrow nest or the chink in the dyke by the ferns or the...'"

"Ok I get it," interrupted Maxwell again. "So what else were they saying?"

"Well," Morag started again, "he said he was very, very worried Professor Whiskerton had come that far up the garden and he'd thought we might have to move house."

"Move house!" Maxwell exclaimed. "But Dad says our family has lived here for a very, very, very long time."

"Well, we don't have to move," said Morag getting a bit cross with Maxwell's constant interruptions. "If you would just let me finish. Dad said he was going to spend the next few days leaving a lot of false trails so that the cat would be confused."

"Ahhhhh. So that's what he's been doing," Maxwell said suddenly realising why Mum had looked so worried and why Dad had been so busy. "But how can he be sure the cat won't find our house, she is a professor after all?"

"That just means she's clever at something but it might

not be following trails and smells. She might be great at erm...at...um..." Morag wondered what the Professor might be really good at. "She might be great at fighting," she added after a moment.

"I don't think that would make you a professor," Maxwell snorted thinking this was a stupid idea.

"Well, not fighting then, maybe you're right," Morag said reluctantly. She hated to admit she might be wrong, especially to Maxwell. "Perhaps she's really clever at stalking birds."

Maxwell considered this for a moment and nodded sagely when he decided that this could be something the cat was very clever at. She could have spent hours studying different birds and how to catch them. And that was very different from trying to catch a mouse, she didn't need to be good at following trails to be able to catch a bird.

"Soooo," said Morag turning her bright eyes on Maxwell, "now let's get back to your crazy idea."

Chapter

9

In which we find out why Morag
hates creepy crawlies, and
Maxwell mentions his mission.

"**I'm** going to go back down to the house and see for myself what's in that tin can. I can do it, I know where to go and I'll be careful," Maxwell explained leaning back on the root and looking a little smug himself now.

"You've been once, with Dad, and you had a narrow escape from Professor Whiskerton. Why on earth do you think you can go back alone? It's the stupidest thing I've ever heard," Morag told him.

"Look, I thought Dad would start letting me help him more but he hasn't. He still thinks I'm a pinkie baby. I thought when he took me with him that he'd realised I was growing up. But everything's boring again," Maxwell's voice was growing louder and angrier as he explained to Morag, "I'm too big for playing games now. When we were out together Dad mentioned all sorts of stuff that he realised he should have told me about and he said he would tell me another time but he hasn't, he hasn't even tried to. I'm going to show him that I can do stuff on my own now. If I do this he'll have to realise that I'm big enough to help him with all the grown up stuff."

Morag was a bit taken aback at just how cross Maxwell was. She wanted to tell him that he should think about her. She wasn't that much younger than him and she never got to do anything exciting and she was expected to help with the wee ones all the time but Maxwell wasn't. She knew she would probably never get a chance to go on a mission with Dad, he would never even think of taking her. It would be Mitchell and Mackenzie next. She just had to help Mum all the time.

Poor Mum never seemed to get to do anything exciting either so why would Morag? She realised this probably wasn't the best time to talk about this with Maxwell though, he wouldn't understand. Part of her knew that what he was planning was just so stupid but a bit of her was really envious. Maybe she should go with him? She shook her head as if to shake the silly idea from her head.

"What's with you?" Maxwell asked, he'd calmed down a little now after his rant. "Earwig?".

"Arggghhhh," Morag shouted pushing him off the root. It was her turn to get angry now. It wasn't just centipedes she didn't like, it was all sorts of creepy crawlies and earwigs were one of her least favourite things in the world.

In high summer at a certain time of day the sun

shone right into the mouse house through the front hole and Morag liked to lie in the sunshine in the front hall while everyone was asleep in their rooms. She'd been lying in the warm sun one day snoozing when Mitchell and Mackenzie had dropped an earwig right in her ear and she'd been woken up by its tickly legs as it tried to find its way out. Even days after it happened she still thought she could feel it in her ear at times and had taken to shaking her head violently just in case. Mitchell had suggested that perhaps it had laid eggs that had rolled inside her head.

Mum had been very angry with them, and a bit cross with Morag for sleeping near the front door in broad daylight when danger could be about. The boys had been punished but Morag still hated those twins sometimes. And she hated being reminded of what had happened.

Maxwell was laughing at Morag but she was fed up now, fed up with his moaning, fed up that she never got to go on adventures and fed up with being teased. She stumped off to find something else to do.

"Don't say anything will you Morag," Maxwell shouted after her. "Maybe we should play squeezy."

But she turned to give him one more black look and then stomped away.

Maxwell decided to follow Morag to keep an eye on her. He realised that if she was really cross with him she might just go and tell Mum or Dad about what he was planning and that would be the end of his adventure. He didn't think Morag would tell on him but he couldn't be entirely sure, so for the rest of the night he kept her in sight though pretended he was busy doing something every time she noticed him nearby.

He also decided that he should go on his mission as soon as he could because even if Morag didn't mean to tell on him she still might say something by accident as she spent a lot of time with Mum. She might want to show Mum how grown up she was by telling her that he was being very silly.

So the next night when he heard Dad say he was going to spend some time sorting through the stores ready for winter, Maxwell decided this would be a good time to go. He didn't want his Dad to be out foraging in case he bumped into him and then he would be in a whole heap of trouble. The last time he'd been punished for being naughty – he'd tied a small spider to the end of Magnus's tail when he was asleep and when Magnus had woken up and tried to run away it had been dragged along behind. He'd run screaming through the mouse house as he'd hated spiders ever since he got lost during the centipede game. Maxwell and the twins had laughed until their tummies were sore but Mum had been the most angry they'd ever seen anyone and Maxwell had been made to carry out all of Magnus's wishes for a week. Maxwell lost count of how many stories he'd had to tell, how many games of marbles he'd played, how many snail rides he'd given with Magnus on his back pretending to be the snail shell.

He realised that this adventure would get him into far more trouble than that but it was still worth the risk he decided. Every night he had dreamed of that wonderful smell and what it could be. There were times he would wake up with a start because he was so sure he could smell it again, as if the aroma was so strong it had wafted right up through the garden and into the little wood.

At breakfast Morag had given Maxwell a hard stare. He wasn't sure if she was worried he'd follow her about again or whether something in his face was betraying his thoughts and plans. Maxwell pretended he hadn't noticed until he heard Morag say:

"Muuuum," in that sing song way that she did sometimes and this time it was Maxwell's turn to give a black look. He saw Morag smirk a little as she said:

"Don't you think Maxwell's been bored again recently? Don't you think he might like to help Dad in the storeroom?"

Maxwell was fuming, he knew Morag was doing this to get at him and to spoil his plans, but before he could say anything Dad said:

"Sorry son but the storeroom's getting pretty full so there's only room for me to get in there and check everything's stored well. It's important to go through everything methodically to ensure that there are no bad nuts and seeds that..."

Malcolm perked up. He loved to hear about anything Dad was doing, especially his storage system, but Mackenzie yawned theatrically, emphasising the wideness of his mouth and the loudness of his sigh while Mitchell said:

"Dad, your storage system is just so fascinating please tell us again about how you go about it?" But by the end of the sentence he couldn't stop laughter bubbling into his voice and Maxwell and the twins burst out laughing at Dad's face which showed that for a moment he'd thought Mitchell was being serious.

"Why you cheeky mice!" Dad shouted after the pair as they scampered off to play. Maxwell ran after them thinking that this was a good opportunity to make a start on his mission as Mum and Dad would think he was just going to play with his brothers.

Chapter 10

In which Maxwell
makes a move.

Maxwell saw his brothers run out and scamper up the oak tree nearby. He knew it had a little nook some way up from the ground where the twins had made a den. Maxwell also knew that Mitchell and Mackenzie had their own stores in there, their favourite stuff like brambles and acorns, that they'd sneaked out under Dad's nose. Maxwell was amazed that Dad had never noticed but then that was maybe why Dad was doing a stock check today.

Maxwell hesitated for a moment when he reached the furthest point that he was allowed to play. He looked back. He could just see the front of the mouse house and knew that if he heard a shout from Mum or Dad he would be able to run back in one breath.

But it was time to take that extra step. He did feel a little nervous. For a moment he remembered just how scared he'd felt when that big furry paw with its deadly claws had caught the tip of his nose. The thought of it made him feel a little funny in his tummy but then he remembered how exciting it had been too and he thought of the amazing smell from that tin can.

"Time to go," said Maxwell to himself, "time to show Dad how I'm nearly grown up now."

68

And with that he darted off down the garden, remembering everything Dad had told him; keeping under the hedge, moving quickly and stopping frequently to check 'the coast was clear.' This was another of Dad's odd phrases that Maxwell wasn't sure of the meaning but he thought it was something to do with checking there was no danger about.

It seemed to take Maxwell much longer to make his way down the garden this time. It felt as if it had become much further, as if the garden had grown much longer since he was with Dad. Maybe it was just because he was stopping much more often to look around because he was on his own. He was trying to be very careful. After what seemed like a very long time but wasn't really, he arrived at the paved area down the steps that led from the grass. It was very dark. He looked about but couldn't see the moon, he knew that sometimes it was very big and at other times very small, as if a giant claw had sliced it up.

His next problem was that some of the flower pots had moved or it seemed to Maxwell that the space between them was much further than when he was with Dad. He looked carefully at how they were spaced on the stone flags. He was very proud of himself for being so sensible.

"I'll show Morag," he thought, "I'm not going to be silly. I can't wait to see her face when I tell her all about this. Maybe I can take her some of the delicious food that's sure to be in that can."

With a quick dart, racing from pot to pot, Maxwell made it to the wall. For a moment he felt panic rising in his chest as he couldn't see the crack between the stones of the cottage that Dad had used to get inside. But then the light changed a little and for a moment he thought the moon had reappeared. He was just about to squeeze through the crack when he noticed the light was different, it had a warmer glow to it and it wasn't coming from the sky.

With a feeling of panic Maxwell realised it was shining from the window high above his head, the light was shining from inside the cottage, in fact from the room he was about to go into. Maxwell felt himself go cold but he was sweating too somehow. He felt very shaky and damp.

"What if I'd gone in? The Old Lady must have just put the light on, she must be in that room AND she's probably got Professor Whiskerton with her!" Maxwell thought.

Maxwell wondered what to do, should he go back home? That would be the sensible thing to do, but how could he go back without finding out what was in the tin? He knew his curiosity would eat away at him. He could go back another night, the sensible voice in his head said. But what if Morag gave him away once she knew that he'd actually gone on his mission and it wasn't just talk and bravado. He may never get another chance. He might be made to do chores until the winter. No, he had to go on with the mission; the daring voice in his head won out. Though his own sense of safety made him wait.

"I'll wait for the light to go out and then a little longer before I go through," Maxwell thought to himself. And just as this thought went through his head the world went dark again and Maxwell let out a big sigh of relief. He was chilly and he didn't want to have to just sit on the cold stone slab with his back against the cold stone wall for too long especially as he'd heard that distinctive night call that Dad had said was an owl. Another big danger, though Dad had not explained exactly why.

Maxwell felt cross again. He thought Dad was wrong to keep these things from them all, he thought they should be told about the dangers in the world, how else would they know what to watch out for? After what seemed like a very long time to Maxwell, he decided to make a move and he squeezed through the tiny crack and popped out into the warmth of the cottage. There was a mixture of nice and interesting smells. But there was only one smell that Maxwell was really interested in.

Chapter

II

In which Maxwell's Mission goes great (then not so good).

Maxwell waited for a moment while his eyes adjusted to the change in the light. In some ways it seemed darker for a moment inside the house. Outside there was the light from the moon and the tiny lights in the sky, which changed a little every day as the moon grew bigger and smaller again. In here it was warm but very dark and it made Maxwell remember the danger that could be lurking in the blackness. He reminded himself of the nasty smell that would hopefully alert him if the cat was around. What he wanted to do now was to find that great smell. He sat back on his bottom and lifted himself up a little, his nose twitching, his whiskers trying to pick up on every signal and scent.

When he'd been with Dad the tin can had been very close to the hole that was their entrance and exit. Was it still there? He'd been surprised that it had been left lying about on the floor back then, could it still be there now, would the Old Lady have really left it lying about for a week? Mum never left things lying about and was cross if anyone else did. Maybe the Old Lady couldn't see very well, Maxwell wondered, maybe she didn't know she'd dropped it. As his eyes adjusted to the dark his twitching nose got the first whiff of the smell.

"Yes!" he squeaked throwing up his forepaws like he had when Mum told him he could have a beetle surprise for his birthday. But then he froze. What was he thinking? He could have woken Professor Whiskerton shouting out like that he realised. He waited expecting any moment to get a whiff of the terrible smell, a clear signal that she was somewhere around. But there was nothing. He let out a big breath realising suddenly that he'd been holding it for ages.

"That was really stupid," he told himself. He couldn't afford to make any more mistakes like that. Instead he put his mind to his mission and carefully, a step at a time, he followed the fantastic aroma now filling his nose. His mouth was watering at the thought of what it could be. Maybe it was centipedes and hazelnuts mashed together, Maxwell pondered, he had no idea what people might eat or how they gathered it. He knew the Old Lady grew things in the garden — peas, they could be really nice, and strawberries, the seeds were tasty but he wasn't very fond of the fruity bit.

And then suddenly there was the dark shape of the tin can ahead of him. He thought it might have moved a bit from where he'd first seen it but there it was, that was all that mattered and there was that amazingly, fantastic smell. Maxwell could barely contain himself. He'd never felt this excited, not even on his birthdays. This was his mission. He was doing this all by himself, without Dad, without Mum, without even Morag. Maxwell followed his twitching nose which seemed to be almost dragging him towards the smell when bump – something was in the way.

"I must be at the wrong end," he thought, and carefully, sniffing all the time, he found his way to the other end of the can. But that didn't have a hole in it either. He went back to where he'd started and peered at it through the dark. Then, using his forepaws and his nose, he began to feel his way around the end.

"There must be an opening," Maxwell thought knowing that he would not be able to smell that really fantastic, wonderful, amazing smell which just seemed to be getting better and better, if the can wasn't open.

He'd almost given up when his nose reached the bottom in the middle and something moved. Maxwell hesitated for a moment and then pushed again at the same spot. It was like a little door, like the little part of the cottage door that Dad had said was for Professor Whiskerton.

This must be a special entrance flap for a mouse! As he pushed at the flap the smell seemed to come hurtling towards him as if it had been waiting for him and was just so pleased to see him. Like when Great Aunt Maudie used to visit when he was very little and she would bear down on him with her forepaws outstretched and then hug him until he couldn't breathe.

Without thinking any more about it Maxwell rushed through the little door and found himself in a smell wonderland. The fantastic scent was so strong and although it was very, very dark in the can his nose had almost landed in something that must be the source of the marvellous aroma.

He licked his lips and tasted it for the first time.

"Wow!" he said out loud, not able to stop himself because it tasted so good. His voice seemed really loud, the sound seemed to bounce around in the small space and he froze for a moment worried that he'd actually shouted. Maxwell realised that however good this was he had to be very quiet about it even though he felt like charging round the Old Lady's kitchen shouting "Woowoowoo" at the top of his voice. He had been right. Something that smelled that good had to taste that good too and it did.

It tasted of nuts somehow, really, intensely nutty but not a nut he'd ever tasted before. Similar but better, much, much better. And it wasn't hard like a nut it was soft somehow but not soft like a strawberry and it seemed to stick to his tongue. He took a big bite and the stuff seemed to roll around in his mouth, coating the sides as it went.

"Wow," he thought again, but he couldn't say it out loud this time because his mouth was gummed up with this fabulous food. It had a richness, a texture he had never come across before. It was nothing like cheese.

And then his next thought was to fill his cheeks and take as much of this back to Morag. Once she smelled and tasted this stuff she would understand why he'd had to come back to find it. Who could resist this? How come Dad didn't want to come back and get this stuff. It was easily the best thing he had ever tasted. Just like he'd said to Morag, it was like sycamore seeds and sunflower seeds and brambles and centipedes all mashed together. But with added nuts, lots of nuts.

He filled his cheeks, after eating so much he thought his tummy might burst like a puffball mushroom, and then went to leave. He pushed his nose at the point where he thought the door was but nothing moved. He tried again, maybe he'd got it wrong. Nothing. Carefully he sat back on his bottom and with both forepaws and his nose he again carefully explored the whole of the end of the can but nothing gave way, nothing moved.

With difficulty he turned round and climbed over what was left of the fabulous food thinking that perhaps he'd lost his bearings in the dark and he'd come in the other end. But nothing. The other end was solid too. With a growing sense of terror Maxwell realised that he was stuck. There was no way out. He was trapped.

Chapter

12

In which Maxwell remembers the
words of Great Uncle Magnus.

Maxwell sat in the dark, his cheeks full of the fantastic food and tried very hard not to panic. A million thoughts ran screaming round his head, tumbling around so fast he couldn't think straight. He was breathing very quickly and his heart was pounding like it had when he'd been with Dad and he'd been scared; like it was ricocheting off his ribs.

He tried to calm down. His cheeks were so full he was afraid if he didn't calm down he would swallow it all in one gulp and choke. He'd almost choked when he'd been little and had made a bet with Morag that he could swallow a bramble whole. He'd just about managed it but there was something about the little seeds inside the berry that seemed to go down the wrong way and he thought he couldn't breathe. He'd panicked even more when Morag had run away but it turned out she'd gone to fetch Mum and Mum had picked him up by his tail and slapped him hard on his back. For a moment he'd thought it was heartless of Mum to punish him just as he was about to die but she'd actually been saving his life. The trick had somehow dislodged the seeds but he'd had the biggest fright ever and he never tried to swallow a whole bramble again. There were times when Morag wanted to tease him about it, like he teased her about the earwig, but she knew Maxwell could have choked and it was too scary a thing to joke about.

Thinking about Mum made Maxwell start to cry — just a little. He felt very scared and wished that Morag could run and get Mum to rescue him now, but he was on his own. He'd never felt so alone. He was always surrounded by his brothers and sisters and even if he was sitting by himself on his favourite root they were never far away, he could always hear someone squeaking or rustling around. But now there was no one. And nobody even knew where he was.

His breath was coming in funny, juddering gasps now — he felt like bawling he was so afraid, but he was trying to stop himself. He knew it wouldn't help.

"Face it," he told himself, "you're on your own. Now be a mouse, be strong, be clever."

He suddenly remembered Great Uncle Magnus telling him in his quavery old voice that 'Mice Are Survivors.' Maxwell hadn't been sure what the old mouse was going on about at the time. He very rarely listened to anything Great Uncle Magnus had to say but for some reason that phrase, that he'd repeated often, came back into his mind now.

"Whatever happens in the world, young mouse," Great Uncle Magnus had said to him, "there will always be mice. Mice Are Survivors."

Remembering this helped Maxwell calm down. He felt his breath smoothing out again and the tears sitting in his eyes ran down his cheeks but no more followed.

"I want Dad to be proud of me," he thought to himself, "I can deal with this, I'm nearly grown up now. I can do this."

He decided to look for the door again but more carefully this time, so he tried each end of the can. He ran his forepaws right round the edges, he pushed and prodded slowly spiralling into the middle. And when one end didn't work he tried the other. But nothing worked and in the end he lay down exhausted.

Time passed. He didn't know how much time because in that small dark space there was no way of telling. He couldn't see a moon or a sun. There was no change in the light. He'd fallen asleep for a little while just as he had when he'd been waiting in the hole with Dad but he was jolted awake as the can suddenly lurched and he fell back against what he had thought was one end. He was more astonished than frightened at first. It seemed as if the can had changed shape now instead of being long and low it was narrow and tall. He was sitting in the bottom that had been one end and the sides that had been the top and bottom were now around him.

Then Maxwell realised that it felt as if the can was floating somehow. Suddenly he fell over, the movement of the can was throwing him around against the walls. Could the can be shaking like quakey grass, Maxwell wondered? He felt pretty sick as he bumped around inside. He was soon coated in what was left of the fantastic food as he lurched from one side to the other, losing his balance and hitting his head off the top and then his tail off the bottom. What was really disgusting was that he'd eaten so much of the food paste that he'd needed the toilet. He'd tried to wee at the end of the can, hoping it would seep out somehow but he'd had to poo more than once. Although mouse poo comes out in little pellets that dry pretty quickly it was still horrible to find it flying past his ears now and sometimes hitting him on the nose as he and his poo bounced around.

"Gross!" he shouted. But he stopped himself from opening his mouth again as a poo narrowly missed flying into his open jaws. He felt even sicker now and the smell was pretty bad. He wedged his hind legs to the edges of the can and his forepaws out to the sides to brace himself and stop himself lurching around.

It felt as if the can was moving but not rolling or tumbling. It felt a bit like the game he and Morag had played one windy day when they'd been sitting on one of the small branches of the tree above the house. It had been spring and the new growth had made the branch wiry and flexible. When they sat right at the end, carefully, the branch had bounced up and down with their weight. Then a gust of wind had caught the branch and blown them about. They'd held on tight to each other and wrapped their tails around the branch and it had been the best fun they'd ever had. It had taken their breath away at first, but then they'd laughed so much as the branch had thrown them about, this way and that. They'd planned to do it again a few nights later but Dad had spotted them half way along the branch and stopped them.

"Far too dangerous," he'd said, "and what if the wee ones tried to copy you?"

They had found a similarly flimsy branch on a different tree at the edge of their playing area a few weeks later but it hadn't been as much fun. The branch wasn't quite as springy and they were constantly looking out for Dad, worried that they'd be in real trouble if he caught them.

But this; this thing with the can was way better than the branch. It gave him a similar kind of feeling like his tummy was going up into his head and then down into his feet. The can was swinging now rather than jolting about so the poo had stopped flying around and was now just rolling about the bottom, though some of it was stuck to what was left of the food. Once Maxwell had braced himself with his forepaws against the sides and his feet and tail at the bottom, he began to really enjoy himself.

"Wheeeeeeeeee!" he shouted. This really was a buzz, a rush of excitement. He'd never done anything quite as cool as this before. He was really enjoying himself when suddenly it stopped. Light streamed in from the top of the can making Maxwell blink as the whole of the end suddenly disappeared. Before he could begin to wonder what was happening the can was tipped up and he fell through the open end and found himself tumbling through the air, he couldn't catch his breath, there was no time to fear how far he would fall and what would happen when he hit the ground — would he bounce or thud or squish?

Chapter

13

In which Morag finds a really
messy manky Maxwell.

"Maxwell?"

He was lying, a little stunned and more than a little winded, his breath blown out of him by the sudden landing. But he could hear, maybe he was ok.

"Maxwell, Maxwell, Maxwell?"The voice was saying his name, over and over, each time a bit louder and with more urgency. He opened his eyes and realised it was Morag. He could see and hear and although he felt a bit sore nothing really hurt, so maybe he really was all right.

"Maxwell what's going on? Are you ok? Maxwell talk to me," he heard his sister say. Gingerly he sat up and looked around. Morag was right next to him looking as worried as he'd ever seen her, as worried as she was at the bramble incident. She looked a bit stunned too. He wondered for a moment if it had all been a dream. Maybe he'd fallen asleep on his favourite root and suddenly fallen off. Perhaps he'd snored too much and woken himself up with a start. He realised Morag was waiting for him to speak. Her face was a picture of surprise. Mouth open, eyes wide, she waited.

"Well?" she said now becoming exasperated at his failure to speak. But before he could open his mouth she added, "Maxwell, I was just wondering where you were and beginning to panic because no one had seen you for ages and it's starting to get light and Mum and Dad are calling us in and I was just about to give up and go tell them that I couldn't find you anywhere," she was gabbling so fast it was hard for him to keep up, "when I saw the Old Lady coming up the garden holding something so I hid in the brambles and then I heard a massive thud and there you were, suddenly out of nowhere just a few feet away and you're covered in something weird AND YOU STINK!!!"

Maxwell opened his mouth and wondered where to begin but Morag started again.

"No time now, we've got to get you cleaned up and home fast before Mum and Dad start worrying about both of us. Look it's getting light."

Luckily on the way back to the mouse house there was a patch of the Milly Molly plant and each leaf held a pool of morning dew. Maxwell quickly cleaned himself up, with a little help from Morag who'd bundled up some grass to scrub him with. Holding her nose with one forepaw Morag wiped his back with the other helping him clean where he couldn't reach and all the time she muttered:

"Maxwell, I just don't know how you got into such a mess, you smell like the toilet nook and what is this stuff, it doesn't come off very easily but as long as we can get most of the smell away..." Maxwell tuned out in the end, he thought Morag was beginning to sound like Mum. And then he did hear Mum's voice calling him and Morag so they decided he was clean enough and scampered the last stretch home. He was glad all his body seemed to be moving all right. He didn't know how far he'd fallen and his mind was racing with what Morag had said.

She'd seen the Old Lady coming up the garden and then he'd suddenly appeared out of nowhere. The Old Lady must have been carrying the can, his can, that's why it had felt wilder than the branch ride. And then she must have tipped him out. Why? Was it a game? If it was a game why didn't Dad want to play it, why had Dad not wanted to get the fabulous food and ride in the can.

"What a boring mouse Dad is," Maxwell thought to himself. After their adventure he'd begun to think Dad wasn't so dull after all, begun to wonder at all the stuff that Dad knew about things, things that were dangerous, things that were cool. He'd been really impressed by Dad when Professor Whiskerton had come after them. He'd thought he was brave then, to risk going out when he didn't know if the cat was waiting or had given up and gone. But now, if Dad knew about the food and the tin can ride but didn't tell the mouselets, didn't even do it himself, then Dad really was as boring as he'd always believed.

He couldn't wait to tell Morag about his mission. It had been Mega, absolutely Mega. A really Mega Mission. And he couldn't wait to do it again. But Maxwell didn't have time to tell Morag anything, not even time to ask her not to tell on him. He hoped she wouldn't tell on him. Mum had been full of questions asking why was he so wet when Morag wasn't but his sister had covered for him. She told Mum that she'd played a trick on him, taking him past the Milly Molly leaves knowing they were full of dew. He'd had a surprise shower, Morag had said laughing. Luckily Mum was then distracted by Murray and Maisie who were asking for an extra snack before bedtime.

Maxwell thought he would be too excited to sleep but instead he was soon dreaming of his wild ride in the tin can. Luckily his mind had forgotten about the poo pellets flying around at first and his own pee dribbling around. And of course he didn't mention that bit to Morag the next evening as they sat on the big root outside. Morag had been desperate to know where Maxwell had been, how he had got into such a state and how he'd appeared out of thin air?

Several times Morag had made Maxwell go back to the start of his story because he was so excited it came out mixed up and garbled and it didn't make any sense to her. Even when he finally got to the end she was still confused.

"So you seriously think this is some kind of game that the Old Lady plays?" she asked Maxwell when he eventually stopped talking.

"Yeah," he answered, "and I don't understand why Dad doesn't do it, maybe he thinks it's just for young mice, maybe he did it when he was a mouselet but then why doesn't he tell us about it..."

Morag interrupted him realising that Maxwell was going to gibber on endlessly again about his mega tin can ride.

"It just doesn't make sense Maxwell," she said very seriously hoping that her brother would listen.

"You're telling me that the Old Lady leaves a can lying in about in her house in the hope that one of us will get in it so that she can carry it up to the top of the garden to let us out again just for the fun of it, AND," Maxwell had opened his mouth to speak, "AND," Morag went on, "she puts this really fabulous food in as an extra treat. She does this why, as some sort of apology for having a cat, because she's bored, because she really likes giving random mice a ride in a tin can...?"

This time it was Maxwell's turn to interrupt.

"Why would she drop me almost at our front door if it wasn't on purpose?" he asked. Morag didn't have an answer to that question. She was stumped. But she still thought none of it made any sense. She couldn't understand why, if it was a game, Dad hadn't told them about it. Maybe it was one of the many things Maxwell said Dad knew about but hadn't told them yet, like owls and cats and stuff. It did seem very odd that Maxwell should be dropped so near to home but if Dad hadn't played this game since he was little had the Old Lady really been regularly putting this fabulous food out in the hope that she could play the 'Carry a Mouse in a Can' game again, and what did she get out of it? All these thoughts buzzed round and round inside Morag's head like a bee in a flower.

The same subject went round Maxwell's head but his thoughts were full of how amazing it had been and how long would he have to wait until he had another shot at it.

They spent most of the night sitting pretty quietly, their heads full of the Tin Can Ride. Morag had gone to play Hide the Conker for a while with Maisie and Martha and Dad had asked Maxwell to watch over Malcolm because the twins had been encouraging Murray and Magnus to tease him about his tail which was unusually short for a wood mouse. Mum had told him it would grow but he was very sensitive about it.

Chapter

14

In which Maxwell gets a big
shock - twice!

It was about a week later when Morag noticed that Maxwell was missing again. The dark of the night time was beginning to lift and the wee ones had already gone in when Morag saw the Old Lady pottering up the garden again, a torch in one hand and what looked like a tin can in the other.

Morag ducked under the bright golden leaves of a bushy beech tree and watched as her brother came flying out of the can, tumbling through the air before bump landing on the tufty grass. Even though he fell quickly she could see Maxwell was grinning from ear to ear but then the landing left him looking stunned for a moment and Morag hissed at him:

"Maxwell, over here, quick we must get home."

He was covered in the funny paste he'd talked about and there was something stuck to him that looked a lot like a poo pellet. But there was no time for questions. They had to get home and go via the Milly Molly plants again to wash Maxwell down.

"Have you played that trick on your brother again?" Mum asked as they ran in the mouse house. "That's very naughty of you. Poor Maxwell."

Maxwell gave Mum his most appealing smile. Morag

97

felt like slapping him. She couldn't believe she was getting into trouble when it was her brother that was doing the stupidest stuff ever that she was sure would get him into the biggest bother if Mum and Dad found out. Morag was starting to wonder if she should be keeping Maxwell's game a secret.

She had thought of little else over the past few days. It just didn't make any sense to her. She could not believe that Maxwell was right, that this was an amazing game. If it was a game that Dad knew about then maybe she should urge Maxwell to come clean, to tell Dad that he was old enough to know about it because, actually, he was playing it.

Part of her thought it sounded like THE BEST FUN any mouse could ever have, the great food, the swinging around, the flying...and she was still thinking that she should maybe go along with Maxwell next time if he would tell her when he was going to go. "Perhaps it would be good to take a risk, to do something different, to experience a little danger," she thought. But there was something about the mess Maxwell came back in that put her off. However amazing that paste food was, did she really want to end up covered in it, and what about those bits that definitely looked like poo. She was sure she could smell pee on him too when he landed, he was very damp in places.

The following evening Maxwell was thinking of sneaking off again when he ran straight into Morag who'd been waiting for him hidden at the edge of their playing area behind a particularly big grassy tussock.

"You're not seriously going again already Maxwell are you?" Morag said looking sternly at her brother. It took a moment for Maxwell to get over his surprise at running into someone, he was glad it was Morag not Dad.

"Morag!" he spluttered and then recovering himself adding, "come with me, come on. Try it for yourself."

"I'm not sure if would be as much fun if we were both in one can," she answered, "it would be a bit of squeeze wouldn't it? AND I'd like to know what you had smeared on you last time. You always stink but what was that other stuff?"

"It's the food. I told you, it's amazing. I'll try and bring you some back this time if you're not going to come with me, I have been trying but it just goes everywhere when you get thrown around at the start of the ride," Maxwell explained.

"Not that," Morag said, "there was something else last time. It looked like...like...like..." she wasn't sure how to put it, "like poo." She couldn't help wrinkling her nose as she finally said the word.

"Oh," Maxwell wasn't sure what else to say. This was an aspect of the Tin Can Ride that was pretty yucky. How could he tell Morag? He knew she would never want to try it if he told her about the poo flying around. He had tried his best to hold on but it was impossible to resist the fabulous food and not poo as a consequence, especially as he was in the can for a long time sometimes before the Old Lady decided to play her bit of the game.

"Well?" Morag said impatiently. There were times when Maxwell thought she was so like Mum.

"Ok, it might have been poo," he finally admitted, speaking very quietly out of embarassment.

"WHAT?" Morag couldn't help shouting.

"Look, I know it's a bit gross..."

"A bit? Are you kidding?" Morag's face looked as if she felt a bit ill, it had a green tinge to it.

"Ok, it is gross but I can't help it. I have to go to the toilet but you can't get out to go, so you have to do it in the can and then when the ride starts it flies about a bit but just at the beginning. Because the food's a bit kind of sticky, some must have stuck to me and I didn't realise," Maxwell explained trying to make it sound not quite as horrible as it was really.

"Ugh, that's just...it's just..." Morag struggled for the right words, "horrible, it's just THE WORST Maxwell. That's put me right off. I cannot believe you keep doing it. However good it feels in the ride, you're covered in poo and pee I bet!"

"But it's such a buzz! And I'm not covered, it was just one...or two maybe. Really Morag you'll never do anything as much fun as this. There's nothing like it. It makes you feel great, like every bit of you is really, really excited, like your blood is rushing round in your body so fast and, and buzzing. It's just so MEGA. Come on, we could squeeze in together."

But the thought of being stuck in a tin can for a long time with Maxwell and both of them having to poo and pee in there was just too horrible, Morag quickly decided. There was nothing in the world, nothing that could be so exciting that would be so much fun that she could put up with being in a can with Maxwell's poo flying around her ears, or landing in one! She shuddered, would that be even worse than the earwig she wondered?

"What are you two plotting?"

Morag and Maxwell squeaked and just about jumped out of their skins in surprise. It was Dad. Maxwell wondered where he'd appeared from and just how much had he overheard? Morag realised Dad had probably been joking but would he be suspicious at the way they'd reacted? Both of them stared at Dad, their hearts thundering around their chests at the shock of his sudden appearance.

"Well?" Dad said. He was beginning to wonder what they really had been up to. He had been joking but the way they'd jumped had made them both look guilty but of what?

"You...you...you...just gave us such a surprise Dad," Maxwell was the first to recover from the shock and he threw in a hearty laugh that he hoped didn't sound as fake as it really was, "ha, ha ha,"

"Yeah, Dad," Morag chimed in, adding her own hollow laugh, "you just really made us jump."

"Well, let that be a lesson," Dad said, becoming

increasingly suspicious at his children's odd behaviour.

"When you're this far from home you should always be on the alert for danger."

"What kind of danger Dad? You promised to tell me about the cat and the owl and stuff, remember," Maxwell reminded him.

Dad looked concerned that Maxwell had mentioned these things in front of his younger sister but he also realised that he had told his son that he would explain about these dangers, but this, he decided, was not the time.

"Not just now Maxwell," Dad noticed his eldest son exchange a look with his sister. "I'm busy at the moment but we will talk about it soon. Maybe you should know about these things now too Morag. Winter will be upon us soon and there will be plenty of time to talk about these things. But I must be off now, and I think you two should get a bit nearer to the house."

As Dad disappeared again Morag and Maxwell both breathed a huge sigh of relief. Maxwell was delighted that Dad didn't seem to have heard them talking and Morag was glad too because Maxwell would blame her forever for getting him into trouble and spoiling his fun.

"You can't go now," Morag said, "You don't know where Dad's gone to, maybe he's just waiting to see what we do next."

Reluctantly Maxwell realised she was right. For all he knew Dad might be lurking nearby, even if he wasn't suspicious he might just be waiting to see if they did as they were told and go back towards the house. He felt very, very cross about it.

"If you hadn't stopped me I'd have been well on my way," Maxwell hissed at his sister.

"If I hadn't stopped you, you might have been caught red handed by Dad," she hissed back. "He may have just come from that direction, what if you'd run straight into him not me?"

The fact that she was right again made Maxwell feel even angrier. They both made their way back towards the mouse house but then with a furious look at each other they headed off in opposite directions. Neither wanted to spend any more time in each other's company.

Chapter

15

In which Mum gets organised
and Maxwell goes missing.

The next few nights were busy ones for the mouse household. Mum felt they needed to be better prepared for the coming winter. Now Mhairi was a little older Mum could leave her with Dad so she was free to organise the gathering of extra bedding material. All the mouselets helped as even the youngest ones could gather in soft things that would help to keep them warm and cosy during the cold months ahead. Dry leaves and mosses, scraps of sheep fleece that had drifted into the wood from the field behind, soft lichens, empty seed heads, the tops of cotton grass were all bundled into one of the many empty rooms inside the mouse house ready to be used when the weather changed.

Mum put Morag and Maxwell in charge of organising Mitchell and Magnus – she always felt it was better to separate the twins when they were doing chores – into creating a huge pile of dry leaves next to the entrance to the house. As the leaves and branches that helped to disguise the entrance would die back in the winter it was important to have something else ready to help hide the small hole.

Meals were a bit odd for a few days as Dad was in charge of putting together the food each day. His taste was a bit different to Mums so there were a few unusual combinations. Mum liked hips and berries in the autumn while Dad preferred beech nuts and beetles.

It was only when Mum felt that everything was ready for winter that the mouselets were once again free to play. They enjoyed the business of their work with Mum but it was nice to get back to having free time. Maxwell, particularly, had been growing impatient over the last day or two. Morag thought he seemed to be very twitchy. He seemed to snap a lot, especially at the really young ones like Magnus and Maisie. He seemed to get increasingly cross if they dropped things or sometimes stopped to roll around on the softness of the sheep wool. More than once Mum had told him to be a bit kinder as they were doing their best.

Morag wasn't surprised that on their first night off from helping Mum, Maxwell went missing. She'd looked for him at his favourite tree root and run around the limit of their play area. She'd searched behind logs, in nooks and crannies in the trees but after a long time had passed she realised he must have gone to play the Tin Can Game again.

There had been a few times when they'd all been

working with Mum that she thought about confiding in her about what Maxwell was doing but she'd never been alone with her. Morag still felt very torn about the whole thing. It did sound amazing, more fun even than the springy branch swing, but there was something about it that didn't feel right. It wasn't just the poo situation which was just gross, Morag still couldn't work out why the Old Lady would want to play this game, what was in it for her apart from a walk up the garden in the chilly darkness of an early autumnal morning. Mum had told Morag that people actually liked to be up and about during the day and most of them slept at night. So why would the Old Lady want to play a game with a young mouse when most people were still asleep? It just didn't make any sense.

Morag passed the time playing Squeezy by herself and Hide and Seek with Maisie and Magnus before taking them inside for bed. She helped Mum settle Martha and Mhairi down and then checked the boys' room to see if Maxwell was back. Malcolm and Murray were listening to Mitchell and Mackenze talking about their adventures that night, where they'd been and what they'd been up to. According to the twins they'd visited the moon by climbing a spider thread and they'd met a giant spider at the top that had tried to eat them. Luckily Magnus was fast asleep, he'd have had terrible nightmares if he'd heard that story.

None of them had seen Maxwell all night and Morag began to worry that he had gone to play his game again. She went back out, telling Mum she wouldn't be long she needed to fetch something she'd left outside. She ran around her familiar checking route, Maxwell's root then she circled the mouse house at the furthest limit that she dared. There was no sign of him. Morag went and hid near the spot where Maxwell usually landed from the can and waited. And waited. And waited.

She was woken sharply by the sound of someone calling her. It was almost light and Morag was shocked that she'd fallen asleep. There was still no sign of Maxwell and now she was putting herself in danger.

"Morag, Morag," it was Dad, "Maxwell, Morag, where are you?" His voice became increasingly concerned with each call.

"Dad, Dad, I'm over here," Morag answered popping out from her hiding place. She saw relief and then a cross look come over Dad's face.

"What do you think you're doing? Dawn's coming, you know you should be back home. It's dangerous for us to be out now. Where's Maxwell?" Dad asked her.

Morag struggled to find the words. Before they could make their way onto her tongue Dad spoke again.

"Morag, what's going on? Where is Maxwell?" His voice changing again from cross back to concern.

Morag still couldn't speak but Dad quickly led her back to the mouse house, watching all the time for danger, his head darting from one side to the other and then looking back, scampering from one clump of grass to a pile of sticks, to a bush, keeping under cover, his ears swivelling, his whiskers twitching. When they were safely home Dad turned again to Morag and she knew it was time to tell Dad everything.

Chapter

16

In which the Tin Can Ride
goes badly wrong.

Maxwell had waited, and waited, and waited. And then waited again. He'd eaten all the yummy paste and he'd had to go to the toilet lots of times and he was very thirsty. Something wasn't right.

He was beginning to feel very panicky when the can finally moved. But instead of being lifted into the air the can jolted suddenly to one side. Maxwell was thrown off his feet. As he struggled to get back up the can jerked again, this time in the other direction. Maxwell lost his feet again and tumbled on his side. Over the great smell of the nutty food and the not so great smell of his poos and wees Maxwell realised there was another smell. A horrible, stinky stench that he recognised at once. Cat. It must be Professor Whiskerton.

Maxwell felt very cold as if someone had dunked him in an icy pool. He shivered. Even though his tummy was full it suddenly felt very empty. It was as if he couldn't breathe, didn't want to breathe because he didn't want to smell the horrible pong. Much more horrible and much more pongy than the smell of his poos.

The loud rhythmic breathing purring sound he'd heard when he was with Dad in the bolt hole seeped inside the can. A soft steady noise that let Maxwell know that just beyond the flap, that he could get in through but not out of, was a nose. And behind the nose, he assumed there were jaws with sharp, sharp teeth. Every few moments the can was made to jerk quickly from one side and then to the other, each time throwing Maxwell off balance.

Maxwell felt as if the thick, regular sound of the cat's purring was filling his head just as it had done when he and Dad had been stuck in the bolt hole on that first adventure. It made him feel kind of sleepy, as if he couldn't think straight, as if his head was full of something that got in the way of his thoughts, muddling his mind. It was like a giant bee had somehow flown inside his head and filled it with its furry coat and almost deafening buzzing. He was just about to try and close his ears by folding them down with his forepaws when something new happened. Something even worse than knowing the cat was just outside.

The flap moved, just a little. And then it moved again, just a little bit more as if Professor Whiskerton was testing it somehow. She'd obviously got fed up moving the can from side to side. She'd obviously worked out that he was inside. The purring seemed to get louder,

113

it seemed to vibrate right through Maxwell from his whiskers through to the tip of his tail. And then suddenly…SMASH!

A paw flew in through the flap missing Maxwell's nose by a whisker. He pressed himself as far back into the can as he could even though he was so frightened he felt almost stuck to the spot. As he tried to make himself as small as he could the paw with it's sharp, sharp claws flew towards him again. Again it missed him, but only just. He couldn't get any further back, couldn't make himself any smaller but the cat seemed to be reaching further and further into the can each time it punched through the flap.

Maxwell regretted everything: playing the Tin Can Game, being mean to his brothers and sisters, thinking Dad was dull. Maxwell had never felt so sorry in all his life. He didn't know what he'd ever done to this cat and he wished his Dad had told him why cats were so dangerous. But from what was happening Maxwell knew that this cat was not trying to shake his hand or invite him out to play. He knew that the next strike through the flap would reach him, knew that those sharp claws would slice through him. And then he really would be sorry, sorry for the last time ever. Maxwell closed his eyes tight not wanting to see the claws as they came for him. He tried to remember how happy he'd been playing marbles with Dad and Mitchell and Mackenzie and Maisie, playing squeezy with Morag, seeing baby Mhairi with Mum when...SMASH!

The paw came punching through the flap, the claws outstretched ready to tear at whatever it could reach of Maxwell. And then stopped.

There was a horrible yowling sound. This screeching angry noise made his ears hurt. It seemed to travel right down his spine making his hair stand on end. Opening his eyes wide he could see that the paw had gone, pulled back just before it had scythed through him.

Before he could think the flap opened again. Maxwell ducked back cowering as far as he could at the back of the can. But it wasn't the claw.

"Maxwell, Maxwell. Are you in there?"

It was Morag's voice. Maxwell shook his head. He must be dreaming, he'd either fallen asleep or the cat had got him and he'd gone to that faraway place where all his relatives lived that he didn't see any more.

"For goodness sake Maxwell, if you're in there come out now. I can't hold this open for long."

He didn't need to be asked again. He felt his heart leap and tears spring to his eyes. Could it really by Morag, and if it was, where was the CAT? He squeezed his nose through the gap in the flap and pushed his way out. Despite the danger they were in he saw Morag wrinkle her nose and he knew he must smell terrible.

"What, what..." Maxwell started. But Morag interrupted.

"No time to explain," she hissed, "Dad said we had to head straight out, don't look back." And with that she led Maxwell along the edge of the wall and then back through the tiny gap that he had first come through with Dad weeks before.

Outside it was getting light and they darted as fast as they could from plant pot to plant pot across the flat stones. As they reached the steps that divided the paving stones from the grass beyond Maxwell pulled Morag's tail to stop her from running on. They crouched in a little gap between the big stones of the dyke next to the steps.

"Dad said don't look back, we mustn't stop, we've got to run," Morag gasped.

"But where is Dad, where did Professor Whiskerton go?" Maxwell was breathless and frightened too.

"He's back there," Morag said, her voice breaking and her big brown eyes filling with tears. "He bit her tail and then ran. That was the plan, to distract her while I got you out."

"We can't leave him," Maxwell wailed choking back his own tears.

"Dad said we had to run, to save ourselves and not to look back. He made me promise Maxwell, he made me promise to get you safely home," Morag began to cry. "We have to go."

"I just can't do it Morag," Maxwell said, "I have to go back."

Before Morag had a chance to argue with him Maxwell scuttled back across the flat stones, darting from pot to pot and despite his sister managing to grab the end of this tail he squeezed back through the gap and a moment later they both popped out, one close behind the other, into the house again.

"What now Maxwell?" Morag whispered.

Chapter

17

In which Morag comes up
with a rescue plan.

Maxwell and Morag had never felt so frightened. Not ever. Things had, of course, scared them before, made them jump or worried them but nothing like this, not even the bramble incident. Knowing they were in so much danger and not knowing what had happened to Dad made them absolutely terrified beyond anything.

They both felt acutely aware of everything as if every sound was louder than usual. They could hear and feel their hearts thudding, as if just sitting there not moving was the noisiest thing they'd ever done. They listened for some clue about what had happened to Dad, their ears moving trying to tune in.

Nothing had ever been this quiet before. They were so used to the noise of the mouse house, the squeaking of their brothers and sisters. Outside there was the wind in the trees, the rustle of the grasses, the creak of branches, the birds singing as the sun began to rise. It was as if this silence was deafening. Then despite the BOOM, THUD, BOOM of their heart beats and the gasping of their quick breaths, they began to hear sounds in the room. There was a TICK, TOCK, TICK, TOCK. A DRIP, DRIP, DRIP. And then they both heard it. Another sound. A SWISH, SWISH, SWISH, SWISH.

Morag and Maxwell looked at each other. They were not used to being out in the daylight and although the sun was just rising it was as if everything was incredibly bright, too bright. Despite being able to see across part of the room they couldn't work out what was making that noise.

They'd both felt frozen with fear but now they began to thaw a little and Morag whispered: "Follow me." She began to edge around the room, running a little and then stopping, running again and then stopping to listen.

SWISH, SWISH, SWISH, SWISH.

Edging carefully along the wall running round things that got in the way, they came to part of the room with lots of things in it. It was a bit like a small wood with very slender saplings all the same regular shape with what they assumed were big dark branches overhead.

As they quietly crept forward the regular swish, swish sound seemed to get louder. And then, on the far side of the room beyond all the chunky poles they could see what was making the sound.

"It's Professor Whiskerton," Morag moved her mouth silently in an exaggerated way though Maxwell knew exactly what she'd said. He'd never seen the cat before, only her paw with its terrible sharp claws.

She was big, bigger than he'd expected and she was a golden orange like some of the summer flowers but with creamy colours running through her coat. Her hair was much longer than he'd ever seen on another creature. It seemed to fluff out. And then there was the tail.

The long fluffy tail was moving in a steady rhythm from side to side as if she was softly sweeping the floor over and over again. As they watched she began to make that deep regular purring sound, the noise that vibrated and seeped inside them, hypnotised them into feeling calm somehow and very sleepy.

"Where's Dad?" Maxwell mouthed to his sister trying not to make a sound. They had hidden behind one of the poles that was like the stiff leg of something.

"She must have him trapped somewhere," Morag hissed back. But although she was as quiet as she could possibly be they realised that the purring had stopped.

Maxwell slowly looked around the big leg thing to see what the cat was doing. Her tail still swished from side to side but her ears were now flicking about as if she was listening. He brought his head back round to Morag and without saying another word he ran back the way they'd come and tucked in tight against the wall. Morag was right behind him.

"Can't talk that close to the cat," he whispered as quietly as he could. "We need a plan."

Morag and Maxwell sat and looked at each other, looked away, looked back, looked at their forepaws, at the floor, up in the air, and thought, and thought as hard as they could. 'What are we going to do?' Maxwell wondered. It had been a blind but foolish bravery that had brought him back into the house to look for Dad, he realised that now but he hadn't thought it all through.

Suddenly Morag, who had looked sadder and more sorry than Maxwell had ever seen her, brightened up. Her big brown eyes shone. "She's thought of a great plan," Maxwell thought.

"I'm going to do like Dad did to get you out of the can. I'm going to creep up behind the Professor, jump on her tail and then run round through all those big legs," she said quietly and very seriously. Maxwell was astonished. He'd been expecting something very clever and complex from his sister but this was a stupid plan.

But before he could say so she added: "And you're going to find Dad and run for the gap. I'll meet you there."

Maxwell stared at Morag waiting for there to be something else. She had to be joking.

"Are you bonkers?" he finally said realising that Morag didn't have anything to add to her idea. "What kind of plan is that? I could have come up with that. That's how we've ended up here like this."

"I don't know what else we can do Maxwell," Morag answered. And the brightness of her face seeped away again as she realised her plan wasn't very good, in fact if she was honest with herself, it was rubbish. "We either go home like Dad told us to or we try this or..."

"Yes?" asked Maxwell hopefully.

"You think of something," Morag added.

Maxwell slumped. He had to admit that although it was a dangerous and silly plan it was all they had. If they had more time he thought he could probably come up with a great plan, a Mega plan but right now he couldn't think of anything only how scared he felt and how worried he was about what might be happening right now to Dad. They didn't have time to wait for a better plan; they had to do something.

"Ok," he said, "but I'm going to do the running, I'm faster than you."

"No you're not," Morag started but then realised this wasn't a good time to get into one of her big fights with her brother about who was better at stuff, but she added, "Ok, you are faster but I'm nippier, I'll be able to swerve through those leg things, I should be able to distract the Professor while you get Dad."

"Ok," said Maxwell for once not wanting to waste time arguing. "Let's do it."

Morag made her way back round the edge of the floor, Maxwell right behind her. They hesitated for a moment, looked at each other and each took a deep breath then scampered through the legs and towards that swishing tail.

The Professor was purring again, the sound so loud and regular that it was as if they could see the air shimmering like it did on very hot summer days. Morag realised that she had to push on and try to switch off from that sound which made her want to cuddle up in the cat's warm fur and snuggle down for a snooze.

"Snap out of it," a voice said in her ear. It was Maxwell. But the squeak of his voice had been like finding a biting ant in the middle of soft bed of grass. Morag was alert again but the Professor had heard him and the purring had stopped.

Morag didn't have to jump on the swishing tail. The cat had turned and seen them and moving faster than they'd ever seen anything move before she pounced.

"RUUUUUUNNNNNN," Maxwell screamed. Morag ran one way and her brother the other. Both of them thought they heard the sharp sound of the cat's claws swishing through the air close behind them.

Maxwell zig zagged crazily like Dad had shown him on their first adventure. It seemed a long time ago when they'd come looking for cheese as a treat for Mum. For a fleeting moment Maxwell thought about Mum and felt his heart ache. "What had he done?" he thought, "would any of them see Mum again?"

He couldn't stop to think. He ran this way and that way through the legs, dashing round and through. He had no idea if the cat had followed him or whether she was now hurtling after his sister or even if Dad knew what was happening. Maybe he'd hidden somewhere and was just planning to wait it out? He was starting to panic when out of nowhere came a loud shout.

"Follow meeeeeeeeeeee!" It was Dad. Maxwell's heart leapt. He'd never been so happy to hear Dad's voice. Dad rushed past him with a whoosh closely followed by Morag and they darted underneath a rug that was lying in the middle of the floor on the way to their escape route. Maxwell had never noticed it before because they'd always kept to the edge of the room, as close to the wall as they could. It was thick and quite heavy but Dad had pushed his nose under the edge and it had lifted and formed a little tunnel for Morag and Maxwell to follow him into. It fell back down to the floor behind him as Maxwell passed under it.

For a moment Maxwell was distracted as he was sure the cat's deadly claws had followed him into the tunnel. There was a sudden pain in the tip of his tail, sharp like the time she'd slashed the tip of his nose. But then he bumped into Morag's back. She'd stopped. Maxwell's mind raced, "Ouch, ouch, ouch," he thought, and then, "what's going on?"

Dad and Morag were huddled together in this heavy darkness. He couldn't see them, it was much too dark, much darker than the night sky they were used to, much darker even than moonless nights. But he could feel their breathing, like his, very fast and loud. The air was warm and heavy like the mouse house when they were trying to sleep on a very hot summer day. As they all struggled to get their breath back Dad spoke urgently:

"We...can't...just...rush...out...at the other side," he gasped. "She might be waiting. We..."

But before he could finish what he was saying something new happened.

Chapter

18

In which Morag, Maxwell and Dad run for their lives.

Morag, Maxwell and Dad suddenly felt the rug roof above them cave in under a heavy weight. As it pressed down on their heads they moved quickly apart leaving the weight crushing down between them. Before Dad could tell them what to do it happened again. A sudden heaviness thudding down from above, this time right next to Maxwell. He pushed himself away from it but there was no way of knowing where it would land next.

"It's the cat," Maxwell heard Dad's muffled shout, "keep moving, just push with your nose the rug will lift up but don't go to the edge."

"How do I know where the edge is?" thought Maxwell in a panic deciding that if he ran round in circles maybe that would work. He ran on again although it wasn't as easy as running outside. It wasn't like squeezing through the tiny gaps in walls either, he had to keep pushing and the weight of the rug slowed him down. He was just wondering where the others were when, in the blackness, he ran into Dad.

"What's she doing Dad?" Maxwell gasped.

"She's jumping, pouncing, it's what cat's do to pin you down, to try and catch you. She'll be able to see a lump in the rug, that's what she's aiming at but there's

129

three of us so we must try to confuse her. I think she'll try to drive one of us to the..." THWUMP! Dad's voice trailed off as the weight suddenly landed on their heads again and again they had to scurry away.

"Don't go near the edge," Dad's muffled voice just reached Maxwell's ears. He kept running, kept pushing but he was getting very tired and he was beginning to get very confused about where he was. It was hot under the rug and so dark and he'd run and run. He had to keep stopping because the rug sliding over his back was making it feel really hot as if it was burning. It seemed to be a big rug but he just had no way of knowing where he'd got to or where the others were. He didn't think it was a good idea to shout as he knew Professor Whiskerton would hear him and would use the sound to locate him.

Maxwell ground to a halt, exhausted, dizzy and he was sure there was a funny burning smell from the heat on his back which felt very sore. Just when he thought things couldn't get much worse there was a new noise, muffled by the thickness of the rug but definitely a new noise. He stopped and kept very still.

Thump, Thump, Thump, Thump it went.

"Maxwell, Maxwell," it was Morag's voice and then..

"Morag, is that you?" it was Dad's voice.

Out of the darkness Dad and Morag appeared very near him, though he still couldn't see them.

"It's the Old Lady," Dad whispered, "she's coming down the stairs, that's what the sound is. Listen."

There wasn't time to ask what stairs were, Maxwell realised. He listened. The steps came closer and then they could hear the noise of her voice. They had no idea what she was saying as she didn't seem to speak Mouse or Cat.

"She's talking to Professor Whiskerton," Dad said urgently, "this is our chance, while the cat's distracted. She may even pick the cat up if we're lucky, we've got to go, follow me now."

But just as Dad said that, Maxwell felt a terrible pain and he couldn't move. He heard Dad and Morag start to go, but he couldn't take a step. He tried to follow them but his tail was stuck — it was as if it was pinned to the ground and the pain was awful. For a moment Maxwell thought he would never get away and again he felt so very sorry for everything that had happened.

"DAD!" he shouted, his voice was very high and

squeaky, "DAD, I can't move. Something's happened to my tail."

He felt Dad's breath as he reappeared next to him. "Dad, Dad, I can't move, I...I..." he was beginning to sob, "I can't move. Go without me Dad, this is all my fault. Save Morag."

"Pull as hard as you can son," said Dad as Morag reappeared too and they both took hold of Maxwell and pulled. Like the explosion of a Touch-Me-Not plant that fires its seeds into the air Maxwell lurched forward; his tail was free, but it still hurt really, really badly.

There was no time to think. Dad led the way followed by Morag and then Maxwell, scurrying under the rug following the tunnel that Dad made as he pushed forward. And then suddenly they were out, back in the open air.

"Just run, don't look back," Dad shouted as they pelted across the gap between the rug and the wall.

They heard a very loud shriek from the Old Lady as they ran along the edge of the floor and then Dad found the gap, the little tiny gap they could squeeze through and one by one they popped out of the other side.

There was no time to stop and think, just run. They

darted across the stones from flowerpot to flowerpot. Morag following Dad's long tail and Maxwell following Morag's. Up the steps, across the grass and then under the hedge.

Dad glanced back over his shoulder and could see that Maxwell and Morag were struggling to keep up, it was broad daylight, too dangerous to be tired, too dangerous to be slow. Morag was feeling really bad, the journey down to rescue Maxwell and everything that had happened since was starting to catch up with her and make her legs feel very, very heavy. Maxwell overtook her.

"Come on Morag, you can do it," he urged her on. "Grab hold of my tail I'll pull you along."

But there wasn't a long tail. Morag opened her mouth to try and gasp something about what she could see when what was left of Maxwell's tail followed him into a hole. Morag followed too. It was one of Dad's bolt holes.

There wasn't much room in the small space. Maxwell remembered how he'd had to squeeze with Dad when they'd had to use one of the bolt holes on their first mission and now there were three of them. There was a little light this time as it was so bright outside and

Maxwell was just very happy to see his Dad and his sister in the hole with him. It didn't matter that there wasn't much room. Despite the fact that Maxwell still stank from his time in the can and his coat was matted with dried paste and other yucky stuff that Morag tried not to think about, she was also relieved that they were all together.

"We'll wait in here until dark," Dad said when he began to get his breath back. "We should be safe for now. Maxwell, lick the end of your tail it will soon stop bleeding. Mum'll see to it when we get home."

At the mention of Mum and home both Morag and Maxwell had to sniff back their tears.

"It's ok," Dad said kindly, "In a minute when we've all settled down I have something to tell you. I think it's time."

Chapter

19

In which Maxwell says sorry,
and Dad apologises too.

Maxwell curled what was left of his tail round and held it in his hands. About a third of its length had gone. It had stopped bleeding but Dad had told him to check that it was clean. It looked ok.

"What happened to my tail Dad, what do you think happened?" Maxwell said sadly looking at it forlornly.

"Son, I think you had a very lucky escape, well all of us did. I think the Old Lady almost trod on us," Dad explained, "She didn't know we were under the rug, she must have just stopped to pick up Professor Whiskerton. Her foot caught the end of your tail but another step and she could have crushed us all."

Morag and Maxwell shuddered and huddled a little closer to Dad. Maxwell looked at his tail and felt very glad that it was only the end that had gone. He could live with a stumpy tail. He took a deep breath. He knew Dad wanted to talk to them but he had something to say first. He felt a bit shaky and as he started to speak his voice cracked a little, threatening to break into crying again.

"Dad? I'm...I'm...I'm so very, very sorry."

"It's all right Maxwell, well, it's wasn't all right. When Morag told me what you'd been up to I was very angry but I'm just relieved that you're here now," Dad said.

"But Dad, I put all of us in such danger. I just...I just didn't know, Dad, I didn't know. I thought it was a game, isn't it a game? Is it just that the cat found me?"

"It's not your fault Maxwell," Dad answered, "it's mine. I promised to tell you about things that you are big enough to know about now and I hadn't. I kept telling you I was busy, but I was just putting it off. I didn't really want to tell you."

Dad stopped for a moment. Maxwell and Morag waited. There was something about Dad's silence that made them realise they shouldn't interrupt or ask questions. It was as if they could feel Dad's sadness in the air.

"There are a lot of dangers in the world," he began, "and I suppose I just wanted you wee ones to enjoy being young for a little longer. I had to grow up very fast because something terrible happened to my Mum and Dad on a mission and they never came back, your Great Uncle Magnus never told me the details. Maybe he didn't know. Just as we like to catch and eat creepy crawlies there are creatures that like to catch and eat us. You've found out the hard way today."

"I didn't realise Professor Whiskerton was trying to eat us," Maxwell said taking a big gulp. Morag let out

137

a shocked squeak. Dad hesitated. Maxwell wondered if there was stuff Dad knew that he would never talk about. Stuff that was just too sad to think about or remember. Maxwell couldn't imagine, didn't want to imagine his Dad going out and never coming back. He thought for a moment about how horrible it would have been for Mum if the Professor had got them or the Old Lady had accidently trod on them all as they crouched under the rug. He pushed the thought away. Thank goodness it was just the bit of his tail that was lying now somewhere in the house.

"Does the Old Lady want to eat us too?" Maxwell asked, "because if she does why did she keep tipping me out of the can? It was a game wasn't it Dad?"

"No," Dad allowed himself a little laugh. "She doesn't want to eat us but she doesn't like mice to live in the house. Before Professor Whiskerton came to live with her a whole family of house mice lived there. But they soon left when the Professor arrived, well, those that could. That tin can," Dad added slowly, "is a trap."

Maxwell took a very big gulp at this news. He couldn't believe air was so hard to swallow, it felt like a big lump in his throat. He looked at Morag. She nodded slowly and then said: "When you didn't come back I had to tell Dad what you'd been doing. Dad explained it all to me. I didn't think it was a game, remember Maxwell. It just sounded too weird."

"I should have told you about it when we got back from our cheese mission Maxwell. I never thought that you would go back down on your own especially after we'd had such a narrow escape from the cat," Dad said.

"But it must have been a game. Why did I get carried back to the mouse house each time?" Maxwell asked, finding all of this hard to take in.

"It was just chance," Dad answered, "the Old Lady probably thought she was taking you far enough away from the house that you wouldn't find your way back. She has no idea we live nearby."

"But she kept doing it. She must have known it was me," Maxwell said.

Dad smiled.

"She probably thought it was a different mouse each time. She won't be able to tell the difference between us, we all look the same to her. We're very lucky that she uses that kind of trap. I've seen traps that are nasty and snap at you. Your Great Aunt Maudie lost the end of her tail, like you have, when it was cut off by one of those traps. She had a taste for cheese too and couldn't resist. But it could have been her head not her tail."

Morag and Maxwell gasped. They were beginning to realise that there were things that they probably didn't really want to know. This was a lot to take in.

"One more thing Dad?" Maxwell asked. "What is the stuff in the can. Have you ever tasted it?"

"Yes son, I have," Dad replied, "I knew it was a trap because I fell for it once too. That smell is so good but I don't know what it is. I've never come across it anywhere else. It does taste really nutty like a hazel nut or an acorn but it's so soft and it kind of gums your mouth up a bit too doesn't it?"

Maxwell smiled and nodded. He was surprised to hear that Dad had been in the trap, he didn't feel quite so stupid now and he liked that the fact that they had something in common that they could share. None of his brothers and sisters had ever tasted the yummy stuff.

"Did you know straightaway that it was a trap Dad? Why didn't you think it was a ride or a game like me?"

"I knew because I couldn't get back out," Dad laughed.

140

"The flap just works one way, as you know. But I knew it wasn't a ride because I was not tipped out near home the last time."

"The last time?" Maxwell asked surprised at this answer.

Dad was quiet for a moment. Just as Morag and Maxwell could almost feel his sadness earlier, now they could feel his embarrassment. It was like a warmth filling the little hole they were sheltering in.

"That's a story for another day," Dad answered finally. "Get some sleep now, we'll get home when it's dark."

Maxwell and Morag didn't think they could sleep after all this news, all this horrible stuff about mouse-eating creatures and nasty traps that can snap your head off but they were so exhausted that they were soon snoring quietly. Dad lay still between them, keeping watch in case the Professor did show up again. He had left lots of false trails in the garden in the hope that she would get too confused to follow any of them for long. He kept watch for beetles and centipedes too as he was hungry and he knew Morag and Maxwell would be too when they woke up.

Chapter

20

In which Maxwell eats Morag's
centipede, but Morag gets
her conker back.

It was dark when Maxwell became aware of his sister talking with Dad. Well, arguing rather than just talking he realised.

"I am really hungry Dad but I just do not want to eat that centipede. I really don't like them," Morag was insisting as Maxwell blinked his eyes open.

"You need to have something, I know we can have a proper breakfast when we get home but have this as a quick snack," Dad said.

"I'll have it," Maxwell quickly intervened and before Dad could stop him he gobbled up the multi legged thing but as it went down he went "yeeeuuuck Dad, that was cold. I don't like them cold, I like them warm and wiggly."

It was Morag's turn to go "yeeeuck," and she looked like she was going to be sick. She followed this with one of her hard stares. Maxwell grinned in reply, one or two centipede legs still poking out from between his two front teeth. He was just so happy things were getting back to normal.

"Ok," said Dad, "it's dark now and home isn't far away but we still need to be careful. Here's lesson one: cats. Cats are vicious, clever and very patient but they are also very flighty, they are easily distracted, for example if a moth flies by they'll jump after it and forget what they were doing before."

"So keep your eyes open at all times. You've both been amazing, so brave, but foolish and silly too but I'm very, very proud of you both."

Dad hugged Maxwell and Morag. They couldn't remember Dad hugging them before but it felt really good, even if they couldn't breathe for a moment and Maxwell had let out a tiny squeak. They all looked at each other, their eyes a little teary. Maxwell knew he would never think that Dad was dull again. And one day he'd get him to tell his story about the tin can experience.

"Are you ready?" Dad said firmly, breaking the mood, "Let's go home."

Keeping close and watching carefully they darted this way and that, staying near to the hedge and then under the big bushes. Maxwell's tail was sore and throbbed a little bit at the end. But soon they knew they were almost home because the could hear voices ahead.

"I'm going to have it,"

"No I bagsed it."

"You didn't even want it before I bagsed it."

"Mine, mine, MINE!"

It was the sound of Mitchell and Mackenzie shouting at each other. Dad began to laugh at the sound of their voices carrying through the quiet darkness of the night. As they neared the mouse house they could see the twins each with their arms around something, tugging at it, heaving one way and then the other. It was Morag's favourite conker.

The twins let go together and fell back on their bottoms astonished as Dad, Morag and Maxwell came past.

"Thank you, I'll take that," said Morag as she grabbed her conker and carried it away with her into the house.

Mackenzie and Mitchell could hear Mum's delighted squeals joined by the happy voices of their brothers and sisters. In their fight over the great conker they'd found hidden behind the brambles, Mitchell and Mackenzie had forgotten all about the BIG WORRY over Dad and Maxwell and Morag who had gone missing and left Mum in a very bad mood but also very sad.

There was a rustling behind them and out of the leaves piled by the door ready for winter came Malcolm,

Murray and Martha. They'd been playing in a little den they'd built in the pile but at the sound of the whoops and cheers they came scampering out.

"What's going on Mitchell?" Malcolm asked.

"Is that Mum? Is she ok?" Murray chimed in. They could still hear Mum, they weren't sure if she was laughing or crying. They could also hear the tiny joyful squeaks of Maisie, Magnus and baby Mhairi who were all inside with Mum. Mitchell and Mackenzie looked at each other as the news finally sank in.

"They're back," Mitchell shouted (or was it Mackenzie)

"They ARE back." Mackenzie shouted (or was it Mitchell). They both jumped up and down and then all of them rushed into the mouse house to find out about Morag and Dad's Mega Mission to rescue Maxwell and then Morag and Maxwell's Mega Mission to rescue Dad.

About the Author and Illustrator

Jayne is an author who writes books for children and adults. She is very tall, but has fantastic posture, due to many years of yoga. The story of Maxwell's Mega Mission was told to her by a friendly hedgehog, and she felt compelled to share it with you. Jayne lives in a small village in south-west Scotland with her family and other animals.

Shalla runs the village shop, but she also writes and illustrates. She wears her hair in pigtails as she likes being mistaken for a viking.

Together Jayne and Shalla are Curly Tale Books, a small publishing company specialising in quality books for children.

I POINTED JAYNE IN THE RIGHT DIRECTION!

Also by Jayne Baldwin

Big Bill's Beltie Bairns

written
by
Jayne Baldwin

illustrated
by
Shalla Gray

Other titles from Curly Tale Books

The Quite *Big Rock*

Written by
Alan Grant

Illustrated by
Shalla Gray

The Galloway
Chilli

Written
by
Shalla Gray

Charlotte's Woolly Yarn
A Spin Around South-West Scotland

Written & Illustrated
by
Shalla Gray

Big Bill the Beltie Bull

Written &
illustrated
by
Shalla Gray